Tracks FROM Nowhere

A NOVEL BY
SHARON VOGT

PHILLIPSMEMPHIS

PhillipsMemphis Publishing
Memphis, Tennessee

www.phillipsmemphis.com
Rose@phillipsmemphis.com

Tracks from Nowhere

Author is a member of the Romance Writers of America

Cover design: Debra Langford Cupps
Book design: The Composing Room, Inc.

Book cover art: Bill Welder
Photography: Yancey Leethe

Library of Congress Cataloging-in-Publication
Data Upon Request

ISBN #'s Paperback 978-0-9788534-6-4
        Hardcover 978-0-9788534-5-7
        eBook 978-0-9788534-7-1

For Tim,
the love of my life.

CHAPTER 1
Unsated Desires

*H*ank tossed and turned, tangled in sweaty sheets, after spending another restless night. He waited impatiently for the first light of dawn to crest the mountain tops. The air in Hank's small cabin was stifling and nary a breeze blew through the rusted screen window. It was August, 1936, in the coal mining community of New River Gorge, West Virginia. The inescapable swelter was oppressive, like thick molasses. The summer heat seemed to have slowed down time, but the heavy night air held the promise of another scorching day.

A low-pitched whistle blew, filling the darkness with a lonesome sound, as the night train rumbled down the tracks. Hank listened to the distant train and the repetitive trill of the whip-poor-wills. He felt like screaming out his frustrations in his deep-throated voice. Instead, he rolled over with a heavy sigh and instinctively reached for his loving wife Louise. His effort was unrewarded. Before last week her presence would have comforted him, but she had gone, leaving behind nothing but a letter of regret. Hank's heart and soul felt the unfamiliar pain of ultimate emptiness. With every breath he yearned for her in a way that seemed unbearable. In his mind's eye he conjured her every detail.

Louise was a stunning beauty, tall and slender yet supple and graceful. Lengthy copper hair enhanced her sweet, hazel-blue eyes. Although her demeanor was kindhearted, it was her spontaneous spirit and mischievous smile he missed the most. Louise possessed a unique creativity that had made his homelife so enjoyable.

Hank rubbed his blood-shot eyes and knew he had to push beyond this desperate feeling. He ran his long fingers through his thick, dark hair and struck a match to light the kerosene lamp. Ghostly shadows filled the room with unsated desires. Bare feet hit the dusty plank floor, and he stumbled mindlessly into the kitchen to percolate a pot of coffee. His shift in the mine would begin in a couple of hours. Like his father and grandfather before him, Hank was scratching out a meager living. He hated himself for not being able to adequately provide for Louise's needs let alone the frills her beautiful spirit deserved. He did not blame her for desiring a better life. In fact, he felt the same way.

Sipping the bitter drink, Hank decided that Louise had been right all along. Coal mining was no way for a decent man to make a living. The recent news of the Macbeth Mine explosion had caused Louise even more anxiety. Ten men did not come home to their wives and family that day. Hank had appreciated her support for seven, long years, but he knew her constant concern about him was taking a toll.

With lunch box in hand, Hank started walking the dark path to the mine. He had only a bologna sandwich on stale bread and a thermos of coffee to sustain him for the day.

Along the way Hank's logical mind analyzed how he got pinned into this dreadful life he never wanted. His family traced their roots back to Ireland from where they had fled the hardship and abuse of tenant farming. Hank's grandfather, Emmet O'Neill, was the first in Hank's family to relocate to New River Gorge. He unselfishly sacrificed his own welfare for his family. It was a desperate effort to procure a better life. In the beginning, the O'Neills discovered a new sense of freedom in the mountain wilderness, but that feeling was short-lived. There was a dark, cruel side to the deceiving natural beauty that soon became very apparent to the miners and their families.

After the Civil War, America entered a great industrialization period. A railway to New River Gorge was completed in 1872, and coal from the abundantly rich mines was transported throughout America. Coal was in great demand to run factories and railroads that were sprawling across the country. As the coal boom continued, companies recruited more and more resilient immigrants, as well as freed African Americans from the South.

Throughout the long days, the miners saw no sunlight and dodged danger from every angle. They dealt with toxic gases and the constant threat of being crushed or burned alive from fires or collapsing tunnels.

As the miners descended into the bowels of the earth, survival became paramount. Drowning was also a risk if an underground water vein was breeched. They overcame harsh working conditions only to be subjected to long-term health problems.

West Virginia's New River is one of the oldest rivers on the planet. Its rugged white water flows northward and cascades through deep canyons, sculpting the deepest and longest river gorge in the Appalachian Mountains. Every autumn, beautiful foliage exhibits awe-inspiring bright yellows, magnificent deep reds, and burnt oranges. The wintertime, however, brings immense suffering as the miners and their families endured the long, frigid winter months.

To meet the growing demand for immigrant workers, coal companies built simple, clapboard dwellings, creating a haphazard community. These structures were both monotonous and lacking in variety. New River Gorge became a place of misery that provided little comfort. Mothers and their children bordered on malnourishment and were dressed in tattered clothing. Wives kissed their men goodbye each morning wondering if they would ever see them again.

Miners pulled twelve to sixteen-hour shifts, rarely seeing daylight—all for a mere three dollars a day. The coal companies paid the miners in their own currency called "Script" which was redeemable only at the company store. Any expenses, such as tools, basic utilities, or health care, were taken out of their already scant wages. As a result, the miners became indebted to the coal company, creating a cycle of endless poverty.

In Hank's grandfather's day, mines were more dangerous and primitive. Miners dynamited and excavated their way into the side of a mountain, shoring up the ceilings and walls with timbers as they progressed. Hank remembered his grandfather telling stories of how they used mules, not only to pull the coal out from the depths, but as a detection device for methane gas. Before the miners entered the mine, a mule would be sent inside with an open carbide flame attached to its halter. If they heard an explosion and smoke billowed out of the shaft, it was then safe to enter the mine. Sometimes the mules did not make it back out, and that presented another challenge.

As Hank approached the mine, his musings returned to Louise. He remembered walking home after work with an apology in mind over the way he had treated her the night before. Instead, he had come home to a dark and empty house. The only noise he heard was the loud chirping of crickets. He entered their quiet home apprehensively and lit the kerosene lamp to dispel the darkness. Hank immediately noticed a folded letter on their rickety, kitchen table. He sat down and read her words that were filled with love and regret. Hank leaned forward, weeping into his crossed arms and thinking, *How could our last night together have been so beautiful and ended so badly?*

Hank knew the reason why, yet he continued to torture himself with a barrage of questions. He relived their last night over and over in his mind. They had made passionate love, and then she practically begged him to take her away. He held such regret for being defensive and empathically resisting her. He actually wanted nothing more than to leave his home, but he was bound by a promise that kept him tied to New River Gorge.

Hank entered the portal, and his head lamp reflected off the sparkling Specular Hematite. The minerals and prehistoric fossils that lined the tunnel always amazed him. They had imprinted themselves, creating a mystery of their actual existence. These mines had a dark history, one that Hank was determined not to repeat by becoming a fossil himself. He had already lost his father and grandfather to black lung disease. Their remains lay buried in an unmarked grave in the rural cemetery. The wooden, grave markers had long since rotted away due to time and neglect. In that moment Hank vowed not to become another victim. Finally, he understood Louise's fear and why she had been so persistent over leaving the poverty-stricken mountains. The path for his foreseeable future suddenly became very clear.

Hank's friend Joe walked up beside him and slapped him on the back. "Good morning, you scoundrel. You look like hell. Are you ready for another glorious day at the beach? I thought we could order us up a couple of dem fancy rum drinks with tiny umbrellas."

Stopping abruptly, Hank looked at Joe with clarity. "Thanks, Joe, for your sense of humor and friendship. Have a fancy drink for me, 'cause I'm leaving. I've had enough of this miserable life." He turned and started walking towards the exit.

Joe yelled, "Where the hell are you going, man?"

"I'm going to find my woman. Yesterday was my last day working in the Kayloor Mine." Hank immediately headed to see the shift-boss to collect his final wages. He felt empowered being in the position of choice. *A promise be damned. Finding Louise is my one and only mission, and I know in my heart where she might be.*

CHAPTER 2

Pillow Talk

*L*ouise cleaned their shack of a home, even though it seemed futile. A fine coal dust constantly settled over everything. Regardless, she scrubbed while cooking a pot of pinto beans and baking an iron skillet of cornbread. On her nature outing that morning, Louise had collected a mess of Poke Sallet in the nearby woods. She slow cooked them in bacon grease and sorghum syrup until tender. Like most other times, there would be no meat on the table for supper.

While Hank was working in the hazardous mine, Louise tried not to worry about his safety; regardless, it was always a concern. She was unfailingly relieved to see him walking towards home every day at dusk. After twelve hours in the mine though, Hank was so tired that rarely did he have enough energy left for companionship or intimacy. After supper Louise would sing Hank a few songs until exhaustion overtook his body. Then she would snuggle next to him and listen to his peaceful breathing. Louise felt comfort in the nearness of him, but her anxious mind always wandered to another place.

At moments like these she reflected on the wisdom her grandmother Octavia had shared. Octavia was an exceptionally confident woman, who measured herself blessed for what she possessed rather than expounding on what she lacked. She believed that things turn out best for those who make the best of the way things turn out. Octavia instilled in Louise the rewards of keeping a positive attitude. Due to her grandmother's influence, Louise's humble nature and her propensity for helping others became the foundations of her character.

Domestic duties filled her mornings. Nothing was easy—from scrubbing the kerosene smut off the walls, to washing clothes, especially Hank's, which took much more effort. She had to fetch and carry water from the communal well to fill two washtubs. Her arms ached from the weight, and she periodically had to set the pails down and rest. A fire was built under one tub to heat water for washing their clothes with lye soap. The other tub was used for a cold water rinsing. Then the wet clothes were wrung out and hung on a clothesline to dry.

After her chores Louise liked to explore and discover new waterfalls, as they were abundant in the area. She loved nature but always felt small and lonesome in its midst. In the evenings she practiced rearranging old songs while developing her own style that allowed her voice to have free range. Her burning passion was singing and writing new songs. Enthusiasm for her music usually kept the demons at bay; but lately, even music didn't satisfy the yearning in her heart. Louise could no longer ignore the uneasiness and discontentment that had become her life. The truth was she did not belong in New River Gorge and never would. Her survival was at risk.

Saturday nights were the highlight of their mundane week when Hank would tune into the Grand Ole Opry on their old radio. They listened to a plethora of artists from Bob Wills and Jimmy Rogers, to Tex Ritter and Kitty Wells. Louise secretly longed to perform on that stage and had envisioned herself there many times. She yearned for a better life with Hank, far from the area's confining mountains.

Starting a new life would be hard at first until they both found jobs, but she felt there was nothing they could not achieve together. Louise believed that music could be their ticket out of New River Gorge. This belief prompted her to devise an exit strategy. First, she would have to convince Hank to go along with her plan. Her previous attempts had not been successful. She was excited and started contemplating a romantic evening with hopes of finally persuading him to leave New River Gorge.

While strolling in the meadow behind their house, Louise began looking for wildflowers to make a bouquet. Most of them were gone already because of the unusually hot summer, but she knew a shady place down by the stream where some Virginia Blue Bells and Wild Geranium were still in bloom. She picked a nice bouquet and decided to take a dip in the cold, flowing water before heading back to the house.

Slipping out of her dress Louise waded into the refreshing stream. The clear water felt invigorating as the current washed over her naked body. She allowed herself a brief moment of fantasy, imagining Hank's strong hands caressing her and his lips tenderly kissing hers. Stepping out of the water she drip-dried a bit before slipping back into her homemade dress.

Louise hurried home excited to finish her preparations. She used an old scarf as a tablecloth and was pleased with the result. Two candles were placed on either side of her lovely bouquet, arranged in a 1906 Della Robbia Roseville vase, which had belonged to her grandmother. Louise treasured it.

After several arduous trips to the communal well, there was finally enough water for Hank to enjoy a bath in their portable aluminum tub. Louise freshened up and slipped into her sexiest summer dress and waited for Hank.

The unmistakable sound of Hank's boots crunching on the gravel pathway sent a chill down her spine. Louise flung open the screen door and ran to him wrapping her arms around his soot-covered body, wanting him more in that moment than ever.

"Damn, baby," Hank teased. "I love it, but what's all this about?"

Smiling her mischievous smile, she ushered him to the back porch. "Strip," she whispered. He did so and eased into the refreshing water—letting out a big sigh as the stress of the day melted away. While Louise lathered up the Ivory Soap, she appreciated his lithe yet muscular body. Lovingly, she washed all the grime away.

Hank complimented Louise's loving touch. "Oh! Baby, I like it when you do that."

"You may like it now, but you'll love it later," Louise laughed noticing that her caress was enticing his manhood. *I'd better feed him first, because he's definitely going to need his strength before we're through tonight.*

Humble as it was, Hank was so appreciative for her hot meal. He ate ravenously like it was the best gourmet food ever. After finishing a second helping, Louise brought out a bottle of moonshine and they both took a big swig. She kissed him with a kiss that started on his lips and traveled to his tongue. Then she gently sucked and bit his bottom lip. Hank was moaning with pleasure as he leisurely unbuttoned her dress and let it fall to the floor—shed like a snake skin. He deeply inhaled her scent and lovingly picked her up with his strong, calloused hands. With a longing and a sense of urgency, Hank laid her across their bed and kissed her passionately. His mouth was wet with desire as he tantalized her, paying special attention to her exotic pearl. Louise felt intoxicated as though she had entered another realm. She hungered for Hank—returning his fiery passion with fire of her own. Wrapped in each other's embrace, they rocked until rhythmic contractions thrilled them into ecstasy. Afterwards they lay in each other's arms and listened to the sounds of a Great Horned Owl calling his mate. A chorus of frogs and crickets joined in, creating an enjoyable night-time symphony.

Candles flickered and shadows danced across the room. Louise grabbed the bottle and passed it to Hank, and he hit it hard. *Now is the time for some serious pillow talk,* she thought. Against her better judgment, Louise gingerly brought up the sore subject of leaving New River Gorge.

"Hank, I need you to listen to a plan I have to get us out of here."

He looked directly into her eyes. "Come on, baby, let's enjoy the moment and not talk about this now."

Louise would have none of that, so she pressed on pleading her case unsuccessfully. Hank would not budge and she knew why. He rolled over with his back towards her—obviously mad. He immediately fell into a deep sleep and began snoring loudly. Louise thought, *How can he be so damn stubborn and insensitive to my feelings?*

She paced the floor and fumed as the candles burned low. Louise decided to go for a walk as she often did on sleepless nights to burn off her frustrations and help gain clarity. Tonight, however, she looked up at the waxing moon and felt alone beneath the vastness of the star-studded sky. The Gibbous Moon rose higher into the night sky, leaving dark shadows in its wake as she aggressively hit her stride.

Memories of her family came flooding in. She basked in the memory of how happy she was growing up in the scenic rural community of Littleton, Alabama. She had treasured the freedom of hiking pure mountain streams and climbing majestic oak trees with her sister. Their country home was on six acres of fertile land in a valley surrounded by mountains. A railroad track bordered one side of the property. Every night Louise would lie in bed and wait for the whistle signifying the train's approach to Littleton Crossing. As the train rumbled down the mountainside, its vibrations rattled the windows of their house. Before the last car passed, she would be in dreamland, where fascinating people took her on great adventures.

One of Louise's favorite childhood memories happened on an ordinary Sunday afternoon. Friends and family were gathered together to enjoy each other's company. Music was always a big part of that fun. People brought whatever instruments they had, and everyone joined in the festivities.

Catfish and hushpuppies were frying, and the kids were turning the churn, making homemade blackberry ice cream from fresh cow's milk. While everyone was enjoying the delicious dessert, Louise noticed a fiddle left alone on a chair and picked it up. She gazed admiringly at the beautiful instrument and started pulling each string to hear its jubilant sound. The fiddle instinctively resonated with her.

I wonder where these memories came from? I haven't thought of that day in quite some time. These memories were rare as they were overshadowed by the great tragedy that changed her life at the early age of thirteen. Late one summer night Louise was enjoying a sleepover with her best friend Debra. They were being silly girls having fun when someone gave a loud knock at the door. Instinctively, they cuddled together under the covers in fright. Debra's mother Josie answered the door. They heard a man's hyper voice, but the conservation was not discernible. Afterwards, Josie came into their bedroom and gently put her arm around Louise's shoulder. She said tenderly, "Sweetheart, a devasting fire has destroyed your home. Your parents and sister all perished along with everything in the house. I'm so very sorry."

Louise felt disorientated as a surge of strong emotions washed over her. Panic hit her very core as she struggled to accept the finality of her loss. Her sense of security was shattered as she wept uncontrollably in her friend's arms. Louise felt trapped in a nightmare as she collapsed under the weight of the sad news.

After the funerals Louise went to live with her grandmother in Fayetteville, West Virginia. Leaving her school and friends to travel to a new and unfamiliar place created great angst for Louise. Fortunately, Octavia was very loving and nurturing. Her generous influence helped heal the wounded child in her early teen years. It was Octavia who enrolled Louise in lessons to master the fiddle as she continued to display a natural talent for the difficult instrument. She encouraged her granddaughter to expand her mind by studying hard and reading many books. Louise's favorite books were always about adventure and travel to exotic lands. She possessed an inquisitive nature and loved school, excelling in most subjects, particularly music. Octavia inspired Louise to begin playing at community gatherings, where she always drew a crowd with her melodic voice and sensitive touch on the fiddle.

One rainy April night, Octavia died peacefully in her sleep. Louise had just turned sixteen. Once again she felt untethered and alone in the world. Although her friends tried unsuccessfully to cheer her, Louise preferred to be alone. Music and writing became her only solace.

Out of boredom one night, she decided to attend the county fair with a couple of girlfriends. While attempting to throw rubber rings on milk bottles, a good-looking young man came strolling up beside her and introduced himself. "Hi! It doesn't look like you're having any luck there. Mind if I give it a try? My name's Hank O'Neill, by the way."

Louise was momentarily speechless. He was the most handsome boy she had ever seen. Hank was tall, athletic, and muscular with dark raven hair and blue eyes that resembled the color of an October sky. He had a confident air about him, but he was not cocky. Hank had a genuine personality that seemed to draw everyone to him. He made a coy remark that captured her attention and caught her off-guard. She started laughing and he joined in. Louise loved the fact that he made her laugh. There was an instant spark of connection between them that stirred her emotions. All her fears seemed to slip away as she felt Hank drawing her into his orbit.

Louise's situation was becoming dire. Although a concerned neighbor was watching over her, the State was in the process of sending her to a foster home. After a short courtship, Hank intervened and asked Louise to marry him. His gentle spirit was determined to give her the love and security she longed for. He knew the first time he laid eyes on Louise that she was the one. With a quiet ceremony at the courthouse, they were married and moved to the coal mines of New River Gorge; that was seven, long years ago.

Lost in her thoughts Louise had not realized how far she had walked. She turned around and headed back home with a heavy heart. The reality of her situation was clear. Louise knew in her heart that she could not stay another day. Leaving Hank would be the most difficult decision of her life, but since he would not do what was best for them, then she would need to summon the courage to do it alone.

Louise was very tired but sleep eluded her. She lay in the dark room beside Hank and resisted the desire to reach out to him, as that would only prolong the inevitable. Instead, she rolled over and turned off the Big Ben alarm clock. Louise got up and started banging around in the kitchen, preparing Hank's lunch along with a thermos of coffee. He awoke in an irritable mood and dressed in yesterday's work clothes. Hank splashed cold water on his face and went to the outhouse to relieve himself. Upon returning, he grabbed his lunch box, and in an uncharacteristically abrupt manner, he left without uttering a single word. Louise watched as he slammed the screen door and walked away from her—away from their life together. Her breath stuttered and the first salty tear broke free unleashing all her grief in a torrent of raw emotions.

CHAPTER 3

Risky Business

$\mathcal{H}$ank convinced his boss to pay his final wages in greenbacks instead of Script. Afterwards he walked a couple of miles on the trodden pathway to see his ailing mother, Nessa. His goal was to inform her that he was leaving New River Gorge to find Louise. He knew that his mother would not take the news kindly due to her irritable nature.

Nessa was never able to bear any more children after Hank's twin died at childbirth. This caused her to be a very strict and protective parent. As he grew older, Hank resented his mother for smothering him with her unhealthy love. Nessa lived a hard life, which created her thorny edge. She possessed a good heart but would not allow herself to step out of the fear that imprisoned her. Nessa never accepted Louise into the family and was even critical of her. Hank had confronted his mother about it, but she would not change.

Approaching at a time of day when he was usually at work, Hank's presence surprised Nessa. He was equally surprised to see his Aunt Eileen. He gave his favorite aunt a genuine, warm hug and learned the reason for her visit. Eileen explained that she had arrived on the morning train. Since her husband Neil's fatal boating accident, Eileen had missed her sister and decided to come for a visit. She informed Hank that they were actually discussing the possibility of Nessa coming to live with her in Fayetteville. Eileen wanted to get her out of the depressing coal-mining town that had taken her husband's life. The two sisters figured they could help each other and make a better life for the both of them. Hank smiled at his good fortune. "Mother, I came to tell you that I am leaving tonight to go find Louise. She left me, but only after pleading for me to go with her. Now that you and Aunt Eileen will be together, I hope you will give me your blessing."

Nessa sarcastically replied, "Hank, you'd be better ahff wethooeht dat sassy wahman in yooehr life. You're too good fahr 'er. After all, she ded roehn away and leave you 'here alahne, dedn't she? What kend o' wife does dat? She's prahbably already fooehnd 'er a new man by now anyway."

Hank looked sternly at Nessa and said with a harsh voice, "That's enough, Mother. Louise is a wonderful person and you never gave her a chance. I've always tried to keep peace between us, but I'll be damned if I'm going to listen to you demean her anymore. Louise is my wife and I love her. Do you understand?"

Nessa lowered her head in shame. She saw the genuine love for Louise alive in Hank's eyes and realized that she had turned into a bitter, old woman. For that she felt remorse.

Eileen moved over to Hank and patted his knee. "Go find that beautiful woman of yours and never let her go. Don't worry. I'll take care of your mother." Hank had always loved Eileen— especially now.

"Auntie, I promise to do just that. Thank you. I'll find a way to make this up to you." He then knelt down in front of Nessa and kissed her on her warm forehead as tears rolled silently down her cheeks. "Mother, I love you, but you know I must do this. Please, I want you to have half of my salary until I can send more."

Nessa embraced him tightly. "Hank, can ye ever fahrgive me? Please keep yooehr mahney. I've gaht a wee bet saved, I'll be fine. I'll pray dat everythin'll be all right fahr de bot o' us."

After their congenial goodbyes, Hank left feeling liberated from the promise he had made.

His father Emmet Jr. died a horrible death from black lung disease. Before his final breath, he took hold of Hank's young hand. With a death rattle in his voice, he made an emotional plea. "Hank, I need fahr you to prahmise me dat you'll always take care o' yooehr mahther. Prahmise me dat you will do dis, sahn." Hank choked back tears as he agreed to his father's request. Emmet Jr. drew one last, sharp breath and silently slipped away. At the exact moment of death, a red bird flew into the window, and the mantle clock stopped at 9:13 p.m.

Hank walked back to the humble cabin he had shared with Louise and looked around, marveling at how she had always managed to make a loving home out of so little. Without her the positive energy had simply vanished. Hank readied the place for the next unfortunate miner. Come nightfall he would trek thirteen miles to Thurmond, where he intended to hobo a night train headed southwest on the Louisville & Nashville railway.

❧

With a small suitcase in hand and guitar slung over his shoulder, Hank closed the door one last time and began the trek out of New River Gorge. The enchanting moon cast eerie shadows on the foreboding landscape. He looked up at the luminous, celestial sky and said a quick prayer for guidance and protection along the way. Just the thought of Louise energized him as he began the journey to recapture his lost love.

Before midnight Hank saw the lights of Thurmond. Hoboing was a risky business, but the darkness of night allowed him to be stealthy. Finding a train heading in the right direction without being detected took skill and patience. Fortunately there was a freight train preparing for departure. Hank found an open boxcar and hopped aboard. Immediately he knew he was not alone. This could be bad news as some hoboes did not take kindly to anyone invading their space.

Hank noticed an old black man, who promptly extended his hand and with a genuine smile said, "Welcome yoself. I'm Boxcar Billie and this here's my sidekick Night Rider. You play dat guitar, or is dat just for looks?"

Noticing the hobo's firm grip, Hank quickly replied, "Yep, I play a bit."

Boxcar Billie took an old harmonica out of his shirt pocket, and Night Rider pulled a set of drum sticks from his knapsack. Hank offered his flask and they passed it around. As the beautiful scenery rolled by, a brilliant moon illuminated the night sky. A cool night air blew through the large cracks, and it mattered not that the only comfort afforded them was some dank fallen bales of hay.

Billie started blowing a bluesy tune on his harmonica. Night Rider joined in, beating a hypnotic rhythm that complemented the undulation of the gently rocking train. Hank started strumming on his acoustic guitar. They were rolling down the tracks, playing upbeat and harmonic music. A sense of freedom and an understanding came over Hank as he finally comprehended why Louise was so hell-bent on leaving New River Gorge. *That woman was always light years ahead of me in her thinking. I should have trusted her intuition. I'll never make that mistake again,* Hank thought. He admired and respected the fact that she had the courage to leave and follow her dream. Regret always consumed him when he thought about the disrespectful way he had left Louise that morning without uttering a word. She had tried so hard to convince him to leave, and he had shut her down.

The hoboes jammed into the wee hours of the morning. The unlikely trio laughed and passed the flask until it was empty. Finally sleep overcame the raggedy band and they settled into the dirty hay.

Hank awoke early morning with a dry mouth, hung over and very disoriented. Billie and Night Rider were gone with no sign of their having ever been there. Hank was perplexed as he knew the train had never made a stop. When he was young his father told him stories about ghost riders haunting trains, but he never did believe in ghosts. All he could think about in the moment was that he felt rough and needed food and coffee— he had neither.

Gradually the train started slowing down. He decided to get off at the next station and find a diner. Cleaning the straw out of his hair and dusting his clothes off best he could, Hank hopped off the barely moving train and noticed a welcoming sign to Midway, Kentucky. He sauntered into The Whistle Stop Cafe on Main Street and ordered over-easy eggs with grits, country ham, and a large cup of coffee. Hank took a sip of the hot beverage and thought, *There's nothing like a hot, tasty breakfast to restore a man's constitution.*

Hank felt so free and alive being able to inhale the fresh morning air. The color of the sky was a brilliant blue with a smattering of high-level wispy clouds. He could not remember a day so beautiful, particularly since much of his life had been spent underground. The darkness had taken so much from him. Hank realized unequivocally that from now on he was going to live in the light.

CHAPTER 4

One Way Ticket

*P*ouring herself the last cup of coffee, Louise sat down at their crude, kitchen table. With a shaky hand she began to compose a letter of farewell.

My Darling Hank,

Please forgive me for choosing to write a letter over saying goodbye in person. Perhaps I'm a coward because I could not bear to see the pain in your eyes. I am overcome with such feelings of sadness and regret. Please know that I have struggled with this extreme decision, however, I feel this is the only option for me now. I understand the conflict you must feel about leaving your mother. Hank, I respect you for honoring your promise, but you also made a vow to me. Our love has always seen us through many hard times, but it isn't enough to save us now. I pray that we both will have the strength to overcome this pain and move on with our lives. If fate is kind to us, perhaps one day our paths shall cross anew, and I will find myself in your loving embrace again. In the meantime I ask you to please find a way to quit the mine. I will worry about your safety every single day. Hank O'Neill, just know that you are the most loving and honorable man I've ever met. I cannot begin to explain how I'm going to miss you. Your love still breathes in this broken heart of mine.

Louise

After folding the letter, Louise left it on the table. She walked into their small bedroom and pulled her old, battered suitcase from underneath the bed—the same bed where just hours earlier she and Hank had been so loving and intimate. *This is no time to be sentimental. I need to summon all my courage for the road that lies ahead.*

Louise placed her meager belongings along with her treasured Roseville vase into the suitcase. She kissed her grandmother's beautiful ring that she had worn as her own wedding band. It had three diamonds that were Miner Cut from the early 1800s. Elegant scrollwork adorned the sides of the band. Louise had always felt that the ring was a perfect blend of art and history. Regret filled her heart with the thought of having to pawn it. Unfortunately, this was her only means for purchasing a one-way train ticket out of New River Gorge.

With her fiddle slung over her shoulder and suitcase in hand, Louise closed the door to the loving home she had shared with Hank. She took a deep breath and with purpose, started walking down the curvy and dusty county road without once looking back. A picturesque stream flowed beside the familiar roadway to Thurmond. The train station was thirteen challenging miles ahead, but she counted on determination, passion, and courage to carry her there.

After travelling a couple of miles, her feet were hurting and she was very hot and thirsty. She wondered, *Perhaps I've underestimated the difficulty of the trip.* She moved to the side of the road at the sound of an approaching vehicle. A mine delivery truck geared down to a stop beside her. A young man stuck his head out the driver's window and said, "Excuse me, pretty lady, my name is Jake. Would you care for a ride? I'm headed to Thurmond."

She responded appreciatively, "Yes, thank the good Lord and thank you too, Jake." After climbing aboard they lumbered down the road. Their idle chit-chat calmed Louise's anxious mind. Jake was still young and not yet jaded by life's cruelty. He told her all about his lovely girlfriend Jesse and their plans to get married. As Jake drove on to Thurmond, Louise reminisced about her youth and innocence when she first met Hank. Jake hit the brake, stopping at the main intersection downtown. Thanking him, she stepped down out of the cab and crossed the street before the town's only traffic light changed to green.

Louise walked into The Little Pawn Shop on Main Street with confidence. She feared that being a woman alone, the proprietor would try to beat down her asking price. After half-an-hour of heated negotiations, she walked away with one-hundred-dollars in her pocket. She felt rather proud of herself. Although the amount was less than she had hoped to receive, it was definitely more than the broker had originally offered. Tucking the pawn ticket into her bag, Louise made a promise that by the end of ninety days her grandmother's ring would once again be hers.

Marching directly to the train depot, she bought a one-way ticket on the 3:00 p.m. train. Hunger pains rumbled through her belly, so she strolled into Woolworths and sat on the only remaining stool at the crowded lunch counter. Seated on her right was an old man, who was no doubt a poor, discarded soul left over from the dregs of the coal mines.

He looked at her and smiled a toothless smile. "Howdy, Mam. My name is Lefty on account I lost my left thumb working in the mines." He laughed and continued, "At least I still got one good thumb for hitch-hiking."

Louise joined in his laughter. "Hi, Lefty. My name is Louise, and I have no idea why they called me that." A friendly waitress wearing a white apron and a Soda Jerk Hat came over to take her order. She decided on a grilled cheese sandwich with a glass of water. Louise knew she had to be frugal with her money to make it last. She glanced at Lefty with only a glass of water and realized that he probably did not have a penny in his pocket. She then motioned to the waitress to make that two of the same. After the order came, she slid a grilled cheese Lefty's way and saw a tear escape down his dirty face.

He said, "Louise, yee are the kindest soul I've ever met. Thank yee very much."

"You're very welcome, Lefty. Perhaps someday you can help someone in need." As they sat in silence enjoying their meal, she thought, *No matter how desperate I may think my life is, there are always others who are suffering more.* She paid the check and said a heartfelt goodbye.

After lunch Louise had a couple of hours before the train arrived. Across the street she noticed Jodie's, a local clothing store for women. As she approached the entrance, a beautiful calico-blue gingham dress in the window caught her attention. Louise had never owned anything so beautiful. *It's probably too expensive, but I'm going to need a new dress for auditions,* she reasoned. The sales lady introduced herself as Laverne and asked if she could help. Louise answered nervously, "I'd like to try on that dress in the window." Knowing the price of that dress, Laverne delicately suggested that Louise might want to look on the sales rack first.

Louise started flinging through the dresses and stopped instantly when she saw a colorful dress with a bright and bold pattern. It was a midi-length bias cut with puffy sleeves, belted waist, and a large collar trimmed in lace. Louise slipped it on her thin but curvy body and the dress looked as though it were custom-made. *Wow! For this price I could buy two dresses and a much needed pair of shoes,* Louise thought.

With luggage in hand and packages under her arm, Louise strolled back towards the train station. *Buying a new dress sure lifts a woman's spirit,* Louise thought, wishing Hank could see how beautifully it graced her body. Out of habit she touched her finger to twist the ring that had once bonded her to Hank. It was gone and so was he. She felt a part of her was missing. Regardless, her future was beginning to feel possible. Anxiously, Louise sat waiting for the train.

CHAPTER 5

Dead Man's Handle

The hot sun created ghostly shadows as it descended behind the purple mountains. Hank waited for the realm of twilight to fade into darkness across the countryside. Stealthily he hopped aboard another boxcar and was pleased to find it empty. Hank wanted to be left alone with his thoughts as the train rolled through the mountains. His reflections were on Louise. Hank knew that one of the reasons she left was to follow her dream of being a professional singer. After all, he had bragged so often about her talents.

Hank felt her melodious voice was seductive and intoxicating, like the sounds of a river flowing to the sea. Louise's singing was soothing to the soul, yet she possessed a style that was rhythmic and exciting—like she was bringing you along on an adventure. Her sound was a beguiling mixture of wisdom and playfulness. He had loved accompanying her with his acoustic guitar on Saturday nights and Sunday afternoons.

Hank closed his eyes to recall every little detail of the woman he loved; like how she would gasp when he nibbled on her neck. He envisioned how she went up on her toes and arched her back when he kissed her on the mouth. God, he wanted and needed her so badly. *I will not stop until I find her and she's back in my arms again.*

To pass the time, Hank tried his luck at writing a song for Louise. He pulled a stubby pencil and a rumpled sheet of paper from his suitcase. The moon cast just enough light for him to barely see, but lighting was not the problem. Hank felt challenged as mere words did not seem adequate to describe his love for her. Louise had often suggested using meditation to tap into one's inner wisdom, so he decided to give it a try. Hank sat in a comfortable position, closed his eyes, and let the clickety-clack sound of the train and its hypnotic motion soothe and clear his anguished mind. Instead of meditating, though, he was soon fast asleep. Several hours and miles of track rolled by as he slumbered peacefully in the hay.

Charlie, the train's engineer, and Casey, the brakeman, were having a debate regarding the upcoming presidential election. Charlie let out an exasperated sigh and stared out the side window. He scratched his head and glanced at Casey. "Politics and religion are slippery slopes for discussion. Let's just agree to disagree, shall we?"

"You see, when you shut down dialogue, nothing ever gets resolved," Casey retorted.

"I think you're mistaken. To have dialogue you should listen to what the other person has to say, instead of trying to intimidate them into believing the way you do," Charlie fired back.

Casey was Charlie's least favorite working partner. He found him to be annoying because he would not shut up. He ranted for hours about government conspiracy theories and doomsday scenarios. Charlie constantly had to practice tolerance and patience. Casey was an antagonist and loved to create controversy. He possessed a reckless personality.

On the other hand, Charlie was a focused man and possessed wisdom that was way beyond his years. He took his job seriously, but in his off-time he enjoyed cutting loose and having a good time.

While looking out the front window of the cab, Charlie experienced a moment of sheer terror. The train rounded a bend and the headlight along with the ditch lights shone on a large tree that had fallen across the tracks less than a mile ahead. He yelled at Casey, "Brake! Brake!"

Casey jumped into action, pulling the brake hard doubting they could stop in time. He then grabbed the Deadman's Handle and fully engaged the safety brake. It was intended to be used only in an emergency, and Casey thought, *This definitely constitutes an emergency!* The dreadful sound of grinding metal shrieked in their ears. The Buffer Stops between cars clanked and banged noisily against each other. Charlie yelled, "Brace for impact!"

Fortunately the tracks headed up a gradual incline causing the train to lose its momentum. The giant locomotive shuddered and moaned to a stop within a few feet from the downed tree. The train sat there hissing and protesting as it slowly settled into stillness. Both men were relieved that the wheels remained on the steel.

Abruptly awakened, Hank heard the awful sounds of metal on metal and knew the train was in distress. He looked out the side door and saw sparks flying from the tracks. When the brakes locked down, he was thrown across the boxcar like a rag doll. Tons of heavy metal finally came to a screeching halt, and Hank jumped down from the boxcar and started walking towards the locomotive. Charlie and Casey were standing in front of the engine assessing the situation when they noticed him.

Charlie said rather loudly, "Who are you, and where the hell did you come from? We're miles from anywhere out here in the boonies."

Hank replied submissively, "Sir, my name's Hank O'Neill. I'm embarrassed to admit that I'm a hobo on your train, but I know how to wield an ax."

"Thanks, we can use your help. Listen up! It will take search and rescue at least a day and a half to find us. We can't afford to wait that long. Since we're in dark territory [a section of track not controlled by signals], we need to set off two torpedoes warning other trains that the tracks are not clear." Then the three men got busy chopping the tree into sections that could be rolled off the tracks. It was hard, strenuous work, but everyone took turns wielding the ax. After a few hours of sweating and cursing, they finally decimated the tree and the tracks were clear for departure.

Accepting Casey's invitation, Hank retrieved his belongings and joined them in the locomotive. Charlie rekindled the fire in the firebox. He checked the water level in the boilers and added coal on top of the wood to get the fire hot. He then waited for the water in the boiler to heat and produce steam. Ensuring that the pit was free of ash, he performed a blowdown by opening the blowdown valve. Charlie manually regulated the steam, controlling the pressure and releasing it into a cylinder. The pistons began moving, which subsequently turned the wheels.

"Release the brakes, Casey. Let's get this clunker of a steam engine moving again. That was excellent teamwork out there by the way," Charlie said expressing his approval.

Charlie gradually eased down on the throttle. The throaty engine responded and began moving slowly at first, then gradually picked up speed. The three men let out a big "whoop" as the night air came rushing through the windows.

Casey brought out a thermos of coffee, which seemed to invigorate their tired bodies. Charlie was curious and asked Hank, "What's your story, man? A good-looking guy like yourself doesn't seem to be the hobo type."

For the next hour, Hank shared his story about Louise and leaving the coal mines to find her. Intrigued, Charlie offered his help in Hank's quest. With genuine concern, Charlie looked at Hank and said, "What are your plans when you get to Nashville? Do you have a job or a place to stay?"

"No, man, I'm just flying by the seat of my pants," Hank answered.

"My sister, Tallulah, owns a house in Nashville. I rent a room from her because it's convenient and helps her financially. There's a carriage house she might be willing to offer you. It needs a thorough cleaning, but it might work until you find your own place. The main house needs repairs, so perhaps you two could work out something. Tallulah has been through a lot, but she's a tough gal with a great heart."

"Thanks, Charlie. That's a generous offer. If Tallulah is good with it, then I'd be grateful to accept. Man, it was my good fortune to hop aboard this night train."

Except for the sounds of the steam engine, all was quiet inside the cab. Finally, Charlie spoke, breaking the silence. "It looks like we'll be arriving in Nashville in approximately six hours. Hank, why don't you grab the bunk and try to get a couple hours of shut-eye?"

"If it's all right with you, I'd like to watch how you run this locomotive. Trains have always fascinated me," Hank said enthusiastically.

"If you're into trains I can introduce you to the trainmaster, Mr. Johnson. We're short-handed right now, and I know there are two positions available. One is for an engineer, and the other is for a fireman. Ordinarily, we would have a fireman on board, but like I said we're short-handed. Trains are beginning to transition from steam to electric, so personally, I'd go for the engineer's job."

Hank stood, stretched like a cat, and replied, "Man, that would be great. Charlie, I can't thank you enough. You have no idea what this would mean to me. Do you really think Mr. Johnson would hire me?"

Charlie laughed and said, "If I recommend you, he will. In this business, it's not what you know; it's who you know."

With a big grin Hank shook Charlie's hand and thought, *What are the odds of my going from a hobo to a potential train employee in one night? Only in America can you find opportunity like this.* The lights of the big city came into view, excessively illuminating the predawn sky. For the first time since leaving New River Gorge, Hank felt positive about his future.

CHAPTER 6

Goals and Ambitions

ouise heard the lonesome whistle blow announcing the 3:00 p.m.
train. As the locomotive came chugging into the station, she gathered her
belongings and walked to the loading platform—eager to be on her way.
The wind had picked up and debris swirled aimlessly. She glanced down
the tracks and noticed the sky had turned dark from the ominous-looking
clouds rolling in. Lightning flashed and thunder rumbled loudly overhead.
She wrapped a shawl around her shoulders to quell the cool dampness in
the air. The conductor called, "All aboard!" and Louise stepped up into the
appropriate car and found her seat. Shortly after she boarded, a torrential
rain came pouring down, causing people to scurry. Placing her luggage into
the overhead compartment, Louise settled in for the long ride ahead.

Two long whistle blasts signified immediate departure. The brakes
hissed on release, and the train slowly pulled out of the station. Feeling
conflicted emotions of regret and excitement, Louise sighed, *Today is not
just another day. It's a chance for a new beginning. Life is not always easy but
from chaos can come opportunity. I must be brave and embrace this adventure
into the unknown.*

She felt her racing heart pulsing in time with the rain pelting on the
windows. Louise wondered about Hank and imagined him coming home
to find her letter. She felt remorse for having left him, but her plan was
already in motion. Yet the pain of separation was more than she could
have ever imagined. Somehow, the forward-swaying motion of the train

seemed to relax her a bit. Louise sat and watched the drenching rain soak the landscape. Raindrops condensed on the outside windows and fell in rivulets down the panes. *I love the rain. It's the perfect disguise for my melancholy mood. It feels like heaven is crying with me. Oh! Hank, if only you would have come with me.*

Her mind rolled on with the miles as she drifted into thinking about the vastness of the universe. The mysteries of life would always intrigue her inquisitive mind. She had read Charles Darwin's book, *On the Origin of Species,* which explained his theory of evolution of natural selection. She had once asked a Baptist preacher questions about it, and he chastised her: "Child, you must accept the Lord's word on sheer faith alone and never question it. Humans did not evolve from monkeys. We were all created in God's likeness." She would always have questions but learned it is best to only share them with open-minded people.

Louise continued to worry about Hank. Recognizing her anxiety, she closed her eyes and took a deep breath. Tension and emotions had dominated her mental landscape, creating a person of fear; and that is not who she wanted to be. With each breath she felt her worry letting go and peace seeping into her heart. Louise realized her love for Hank would always be with her, and she felt comfort in that. With total surrender of her painful memories, a glorious sleep came to her like a most welcome guest.

Night had fallen when Louise awoke from a two-hour nap. After visiting the facilities and freshening up a bit, she walked to the diner car and purchased a ham sandwich and treated herself to an ice-cold Coca-Cola. Louise noticed a young woman holding a sleeping baby in her arms. Louise saw how tenderly the mother held her child, and it touched her deeply. She longed for a baby of her own but thought, *Now is not the time to be thinking about that. I have to remain focused on my goals and ambitions.* Louise returned to her seat and wrote a poem she might later turn into a song. *Beautiful words have such power to evoke emotions, and I love stringing them together,* she thought.

Louise had only been on a train once before when she went to live with her grandmother. This time she took notice that riding a train is a great way to tap into one's creativity. She felt inspired as her pencil flew across the page expressing her ideas. Life had beckoned her, and she had answered the call. The train continued traveling late into the night finally rocking Louise into a tranquil sleep.

The morning sun came shining into the window causing Louise to abandon her slumber. She stretched to get the kinks out and walked to the facilities to revive herself. While splashing cold water on her face, she remembered sharing this morning ritual with her mother. Louise still missed having her to talk to; she surely could use her advice. She groomed herself as much as possible under the circumstances before venturing into the dining car for breakfast.

The host seated her directly across the table from a middle-aged, handsome man. He was well-dressed, sporting a grey Harris Tweed suit with a double-breasted jacket and wide lapels. A sporty, five-button vest complemented his suit. With a distinct dialect, the gentleman politely introduced himself as Calvin Durant from New Orleans. Louise obliged and likewise introduced herself and shared that she was headed to Nashville. They fell into a conversation that felt both comfortable and natural.

"I'm also headed to Nashville to service a few of my business accounts," he explained. Louise had never experienced the attention of an obviously wealthy man, but she was rather enjoying his company. Calvin gave her a sincere smile that seemed to linger. "If you don't mind my asking, what are your plans when you get to Nashville."

Louise returned his smile. "I'm a singer and a musician, and my ultimate dream is to sing on the Grand Ole Opry stage."

Calvin leaned back and said, "Well, I'll be damned. It so happens that I have a long-time friend, Sonny Reinheart, who's a music producer in Nashville. I believe I have his card." Looking through his wallet, Calvin pulled out Sonny's business card with pride. "Yes, here it is. I'm going to write a note on the back. Call for an appointment and take this card with you as an introduction. If your beauty is any indication of your talent, you're bound for stardom." Louise took the card and thanked him, blushing from the rare compliment given by a good-looking stranger.

"Would you kindly accept my invitation for dinner after we arrive in Nashville", Calvin asked.

"Thanks for your gracious offer. I'm not sure where I'll be staying so perhaps another time."

"I'm staying at The Noel Hotel, and I can book a room for you if you like. My driver could take you there."

Louise contemplated her options. Considering that she wasn't familiar with Nashville, she kindly accepted.

She returned to her seat thinking about the chance encounter with Mr.

Calvin Durant. Louise thought, *There's something very worldly and intriguing about him. I've never met anyone like him before.* She sat down in her seat, holding Sonny's card tightly in her hand—as though it were a lifeline.

The jolly conductor strolled down the aisle, announcing, "Ladies and gentlemen, the next stop is Nashville. We will arrive at Union Station in forty-five minutes. Please check the overhead rack and gather your belongings. We sincerely hope you've enjoyed your trip." Louise was so excited she could hardly remain in her seat.

CHAPTER 7

First Glimpse

Hank felt fatigued after a challenging night but was in good spirits as the train arrived at Union Station. The florid orange sun greeted him as it rose slowly over downtown Nashville. Marveling at the fascinating architecture, he was awestruck with the small but vibrant city. Life was bustling on the streets as multi-cultural people began to carry on their business of a new day. Life here seemed to hum with an energy unlike anything he had ever seen before. Hank thought, *Where will this exciting city take me on my quest to find Louise?*

After powering down the locomotive, Charlie completed his checklist. Afterwards, he invited Hank for bacon and eggs at the station's diner. The hot coffee and hearty breakfast invigorated their tired bodies. Charlie picked up the tab and said, "Let's walk across the street to the depot office and I'll introduce you to Mr. Johnson. Let's not mention anything about how we met."

Charlie knocked on Mr. Johnson's door, and he bid him to enter. "Good morning, Sir. I would like for you to meet my friend, Hank O'Neill. He has just moved to Nashville and is looking for employment. With your approval, I'd like to recommend him for the position of engineer."

Mr. Johnson looked at Hank and said, "Hank, do you have any experience?"

"No, sir, but I'm a quick learner."

"Son, if I hire you, will you be an honest and loyal employee for the Louisville & Nashville railroad?"

"Yes, sir! It's an honor just to be considered for the position. I promise to work hard for the company," Hank replied.

Mr. Johnson looked directly at Hank. "Well, since Charlie has recommended you, and we need employees, the job is yours. Sign this employment contract, and I'll work you into the schedule to begin your training. By the way, Charlie. I'll be expecting your report on the incident that happened on your last run. Also, I thought you would want to know that Casey has requested a transfer to his home state Ohio. I have granted his request effective immediately."

"I wish Casey well. No problem, sir. I'll get that report to you by tomorrow," Charlie said. Thankful for the job opportunity, Hank thought, *This sure feels right. I'm so glad to be here away from the mines. Now I've got to find Louise. She's sure gonna be surprised to see me.*

Charlie slapped Hank on the back. "Congratulations, man. Now, let's go meet that sister of mine."

Charlie hailed a taxi at the train station and they climbed in. The cab driver pulled into the driveway of a beautiful, old cottage on Franklin Road. Early fall foliage was visible on the large oak trees that shaded an attractively manicured lawn. Hank immediately noticed the ornate windows gracing the front of the house and golden sunlight reflecting off the windowpanes. Fragrant rose bushes with lovely red and yellow blooms flanked the windows, and sprawling vines attached themselves to the brick chimney and extended up to the old slate roof. Even though the exterior looked tidy, the property needed work.

Hank caught his first glimpse of Tallulah as she stepped out the front door with her German shepherd, Queenie, by her side. Hank was momentarily dazed when he saw that Tallulah was a very attractive woman. He took notice of her long, brunette hair and emerald eyes that appeared to be as deep as an ocean.

Charlie gave his sister a hug. "Tallulah, I'd like for you to meet Hank O'Neill. Hank is my new friend and the latest hire at the railroad. I was wondering if you would consider offering him your carriage house? In return for rent, Hank volunteered to help with the home repairs that we previously discussed."

Tallulah smiled at Hank and said, "I'd be happy to offer you the carriage house. It needs cleaning, but if it suits your needs you're welcome to stay."

Hank thanked her and thought, *Guess I have a fallen tree to thank for this great stroke of luck.*

"Tallulah, would you mind running to the grocery for steaks and fixings?" Charlie asked. "I'll stay and help Hank clean the carriage house."

As Hank mopped the floor, he inquired about Tallulah.

With a sad sigh, Charlie answered. "Her husband died in a mine that collapsed a couple of years ago, his body was never recovered. She moved to Nashville to be near me, because we're the only family either of us have left."

Hank shook his head and thought, *That could very well have been me.*

After the carriage house was cleaned and fresh sheets were placed on the bed, Charlie left to take a nap. Hank took a much needed bath and lay down on the bed. Then his musing careened onto Tallulah. There was something mysterious and undone about her. Hank thought, *What an intriguing woman.* That was the last thing he remembered before exhaustion claimed his tired body.

CHAPTER 8

Kindred Spirit

$\mathscr{L}$ouise handed a porter her luggage as she stepped down from the train. Calvin was patiently waiting. "Welcome to Nashville, Louise. I'm at your service." She returned his smile, and took his extended arm as they strolled towards Union Station.

Noticing Louise's admiration of Nashville's beautiful architecture, Calvin said, "Richard Montfort designed this railroad terminal in the Victorian Romanesque Revival Style. He was the chief engineer of the Louisville & Nashville Railroad at the time. Check out the high towers and turrets reminiscent of an old European castle. Can you see the bronze statue of the Roman god Mercury atop the tallest tower?" Louise looked up and nodded. Calvin continued, "Construction was completed in 1900 to accommodate passengers for the eight railroads that provided service to Nashville."

Marveling at the exquisite carvings in the heavy, rough stone surface, Louise replied, "Thanks for sharing that bit of history. Calvin, this is the most beautiful building I've ever seen."

They walked outside Union Station and a driver waited in a handsome 1936 Mercedes-Benz 260D Pullman Landaulet. Louise gasped as she took in the chrome and black beauty. The graceful curvilinear design of the fenders along with the bulbous headlights helped create a luxurious extravagance that she never knew existed. After the driver loaded their luggage, Calvin requested that he take them to The Noel Hotel.

Recapturing her composure, Louise said, "Calvin, I can't thank you enough for arranging a place for me to stay."

He quickly replied, "You could have dinner with me tonight, cher."

"My apologies; I'm really tired and would like to just settle in. Can we make it for tomorrow night?"

"Indeed. Meet me in the bar downstairs tomorrow evening at 7:00 p.m., and we'll have a proper drink before dinner," he replied.

🌼

As the driver pulled up to the entrance of The Noel Hotel, Calvin quickly gave Louise another brief history. This grand hotel with its twelve floors is the tallest building in Nashville. It was designed in the Classic Revival Style by architects Marr and Holman. The hotel roof proudly displays a large green neon sign that illuminates the family name, Noel. The huge sign can be seen from the paddle boats that cruise the scenic Cumberland River.

Louise was humbled and felt intimidated by the grandeur of the hotel. "Thank you, Calvin, but there's no way I can afford to stay here."

"Oscar and John Noel are old friends of mine. Louise, as a favor to me, please accept my offer with absolutely no obligation."

Louise thought for a moment about her options. *I'm tired and don't know my way around town. Trying to find a decent place to stay that I can afford seems overwhelming.* She sighed. "I humbly accept your offer for a couple of days until I can find my own place. Thank you, Calvin, for your generosity. It's much appreciated."

He extended his arm to her and said, "Fair enough! Now, let's get you checked in."

When they walked into the lobby, Louise was awestruck. She had never seen any place so beautiful in her life. An elaborate crystal chandelier hung from the center of the room illuminating the grand lobby. The chairs and sofas were upholstered in exquisite fabrics, and period tapestries hung gracefully in prominent spots. Original art adorned the walls and complemented the decorative rugs and furnishings. Louise felt like a child visiting a city for the first time.

Calvin returned and placed into her hand a brass key engraved with the number 505. He commented, "Louise, you can either have dinner downstairs or you may order room service. Either way, just sign your name and room number on the ticket." Gently he took her arm and escorted Louise to the elaborately appointed elevators. Calvin pushed the button for the fifth floor, and Louise felt a bit of apprehension as the carriage started ascending.

The elevator stopped with a jolt, and they stepped into the corridor. He accompanied her to her room and said, "Get some rest, Louise. I look forward to seeing you tomorrow evening at 7:00 p.m."

She smiled and looked at him appreciatively. "Calvin, thank you so much. This is really exceptional. I look forward to the day when I may repay your kindness."

He nodded shyly and said, "My lady, I take my leave. Please enjoy your evening."

✲

Calvin walked away, heading to his own room to freshen up before dinner. He was surprised and delighted by the optimism he felt about Louise. He had noticed how she tried to hide her beat up old suitcase and it touched him in such a strange and charming way. He thought, *Louise is no doubt a desirable and beautiful woman, but somehow I feel a kindred spirit with her. She may be young and a bit naïve, but she possesses a lot of wisdom for her age. Hopefully, I can help her in some way to realize her potential.*

Having grown up poor himself, Calvin understood all too well the transition from rags to riches. He saw a glimpse of his younger self in Louise as she exhibited a sense of false bravado. Calvin recognized her as a strong woman with an independent spirit; however, he also detected a vulnerable crack in her facade. He thought, *I'm happy to provide a safe refuge until she can find her wings. If it had not been for the kindness of strangers, I certainly would not be CEO of a successful company in New Orleans.*

After fumbling to fit the unfamiliar key into the lock, Louise opened the door into a well-appointed room with a view of downtown. She danced and twirled around the room, not believing her good fortune. Then she noticed the stunning bathroom with black-and-white marble floors. What captured her attention most was the attractive claw-foot porcelain tub. She turned on the spigot, and hot water came pouring out filling the tub with glorious water. Louise thought, *This is unbelievable!* remembering how difficult it was to haul bathwater in New River Gorge. An assorted variety of toiletries were displayed on the counter, and she chose a lavender and lemongrass essential oil to add to her bath. Louise was giddy as the steam fogged the mirrors. She undressed and slipped into the hot water and felt all her stress melt away.

Louise had always referred to New River Gorge as 'Nowhere, West Virginia,' because the inhabitants of the remote village suffered immensely just to survive. Amidst the luxury of her accommodations, she felt light-years away from that place. However, guilt still gnawed at her for leaving Hank behind. Her eyes became moist as she held back her tears. She slid further down into the pleasing aromatic water, thankful for this momentary escape and much appreciated bliss. While soaking, she experienced an epiphany—every little thing is going to be all right.

CHAPTER 9

Powerful Tide of Change

*H*ank tasted the last bite of his delicious steak—savoring the flavors. Tallulah had placed wet rosemary atop the hot coals, which gave the meat a distinctive herbal flavor.

Wiping his face with a napkin, Hank said, "Thanks, Charlie, for buying, and Tallulah, for your fine grilling skills. I can't ever remember enjoying a meal that much."

Tallulah remarked, "Our pleasure. Why don't you two have a seat on the back porch, and I'll join you shortly with an after-dinner drink." Tallulah stacked the dishes and decided to wash them later. Her curiosity was piqued about Hank and his journey. After handing each man a whiskey, she took a seat in an empty rocking chair.

"Welcome to Nashville, Hank. Here's hoping that you find whatever you're looking for," Tallulah toasted.

"Thanks, I feel fortunate to be here. I'm grateful to you, Charlie, for referring me. This job means a lot."

"Glad to have helped. I've got a good feeling about you, Hank. You're all right in my book. Hey! I've got a joke for y'all," Charlie announced.

An old man walks into a bar and orders a beer. The bartender notices the man's head is the size of a baseball, so he asks him what happened. The old man takes a bar stool and tells the story about how his ship was torpedoed in the war.

"A mermaid rescued me and offered three wishes: my first was to return to the States safely, the second was for a lot of money; and finally; my third wish was to have sex with a mermaid. The problem is mermaids can't have sex. My mistake was asking her if I could just have a little head instead."

Hank was beginning to feel the whiskey and laughed louder than the joke was funny. Tallulah laughed also and said, "That's enough corny jokes for one night. So, Hank, what brings you to Nashville?"

He passionately told his story. Tallulah tried to hide her disappointment in discovering that he was married and his purpose in coming to Nashville was to find his wife. There was something about Hank that aroused a longing that she thought had become extinct. Being around him for only a short time had made her realize how much she still craved the touch of a good-looking man.

Hank became quiet and was staring out into the darkness deep in thought. *What a lucky man I am. With Charlie and Tallulah's help, locating Louise now seems like a reality.*

Charlie touched Hank's shoulder and jolted him. "Hey, sorry to disturb your pondering. I was just thinking, why don't we go downtown and begin inquiring about Louise?"

"Thanks, Charlie. That's a great idea. I can't wait to experience the Nashville scene."

Hank was enthralled with the city lights. The enticing neon signs were flashing like proud peacocks—a stark contrast to New River Gorge, where the stars in heaven were the brightest lights. Nashville appeared to have an energy that was alive and thriving. Musicians were playing on street corners—creating an atmosphere of celebration despite the terrible depression that had been gripping America. Americans needed something to lift their spirits, and music had become a salve for the soul. Nashville was a mecca where musicians could freely express themselves. Country music, blues, and jazz thrived and expanded in popularity. Music became the antidote for the discouraged souls trying to survive the oppressive times.

Charlie, Tallulah and Hank wandered into several clubs on Lower Broadway inquiring if anyone had heard of a new singer called Louise O'Neill. Each time, they bellied up to the bar and had a shot of whiskey. Hank was amazed at the difference between the moonshine he had been drinking as compared to the smooth Tennessee whiskey. After several negative responses to their inquiries, Hank was becoming a bit discouraged.

Charlie noticed his disappointment. "Come on, man. This is just our first night looking. I'll put word about Louise on the streets. The news will spread; and if she's in Nashville, trust me, we'll find her."

"You're right, let's go. I start my training in the morning. If I keep drinking this here good whiskey, I won't make it out of bed," Hank replied.

Early the next morning Hank was on the railroad yard when Mr. Johnson began explaining the layout of a complex series of tracks. He expounded: "These particular tracks are used for loading or unloading and moving cars and locomotives to ensure the main line is always open for traffic. There's a map in the office that will help until you familiarize yourself with the system." Mr. Johnson pulled out a training manual and handed it to Hank. "I want you to read that first paragraph to me."

Hank accepted the manual and started reading: "An engineer's responsibilities include operating all controls, engaging the throttle, and maintaining the correct speed. It's mandatory that a thorough inspection be made before departure and upon arrival. An engineer must remain alert at all times for obstructions on the tracks. Avoid accidents whenever possible, but if unavoidable an accident report must be submitted."

Mr. Johnson nodded his head and said, "You're going to learn so much, but that's it in a nutshell. Probably the most important piece of advice I can give you is the importance of following schedules. Let's go climb aboard locomotive number nine and start your training. Any questions?"

Hank confidently replied, "No, sir! With your help, I'm ready to roll."

"That's good to hear. Oh! Hank, I forgot to mention that Charlie got called out today. The Chattanooga Yard is short-handed and needed help over there. He should be back in a few days. That means by the time he gets back, I want you up and running."

Hank was excited about his first day of training. When his shift was over, he hitched a ride home to start repairing the leaky roof. As he walked into the yard, Queenie came running to him and rolled over for a belly rub.

"Hank, I do believe that Queenie is getting attached to you," Tallulah said.

"Queenie's a great dog, but I believe I'm the one who's getting attached."

Tallulah invited Hank inside for a sandwich and a glass of sweet tea before he began working. Afterwards, he climbed up the ladder and took special notice of the sunshine and warm breezes blowing. He offered a moment of thanks for not being in the stifling, dark mine. Hank felt a powerful tide of change was at play, yet he welcomed it even as it altered his perception of life.

In a matter of days, Hank had settled into a comfortable routine, training at the station and working on Tallulah's house in the afternoons. After he repaired the roof, Hank started building new steps for the back porch. One evening after driving the final nail, he decided to take a shower and go downtown looking for Louise. Hank walked out the door with his guitar slung over his shoulder. He had met some talented fellows from down in Alabama whose musical style he really liked. They too were now in on the quest to locate Louise. Word had spread on the streets and in the downtown clubs. *It's just a matter of time until I find you Louise,* he thought.

CHAPTER 10

Kismet

Louise awoke from a nightmare. She had been searching frantically for Hank in the rubble of a collapsed mine. She felt disoriented waking in the opulence of her new surroundings. To escape her anxiety, Louise took a quick shower, letting the water wash away her fears.

After enjoying breakfast from room service, she slipped into one of her new dresses and set out to explore downtown. Her first priority was finding a place to rent. She did not feel comfortable taking advantage of Calvin's generosity. Louise also realized she would need more appropriate attire for an audition than the dresses she had bought in Thurmond. Turning the corner on Second Avenue, Louise noticed a sign announcing *Hazel Bleu's Ladies' Boutique.* She opened the ornately carved door of the intriguing shop and walked inside where she was greeted by an attractive woman.

"Hello, my name's Sadie. Just ask if you need help." While perusing through the racks, Louise came upon a curve-hugging black dress with a cinched waist and accented with white-satin trim. Sadie saw her admiring the dress and asked, "Why don't you slip it on?"

Louise felt a bit embarrassed as she hung the dress back on the rack. "This is an incredible dress, but I'm afraid I really can't afford it. I just came into town yesterday on the train, and I'm looking for a singing gig," she explained.

Sadie replied, "Oh, Honey! I totally understand what it's like being new in town and looking for a job. Perhaps I can help. The owner told me to mark down these dresses to fifty percent off to make room for a new shipment. I bet you would look gorgeous in this dress." Standing in front of a full-length mirror, Louise could not help but smile as she gazed at her reflection.

"Louise, you have nice skin, but I can enhance your natural beauty with products from our cosmetic line. It won't cost a thing for me to show you what applying a small touch of makeup can do. Also, I'll give you some samples so you can look your best at a job interview."

Having never worn makeup before, Louise was a little hesitant but agreed to give it a try. Sadie retrieved the cosmetics and applied them sparingly. The dress and makeup gave Louise a newfound confidence that she would soon find a job. She bought the dress thinking to herself, *This dress is an investment in my future.*

Louise and Sadie shared stories of how they came to Nashville. Louise thought, *Sadie's really nice and has been a great help. Perhaps we could be friends.*

As if reading her mind, Sadie suggested, "Would you like to come to my place one night for dinner? I know from personal experience that it can be lonely when you're new in town. Louise, I admire your courage and would like to get to know you better."

"Yes, I would love that. I'm temporarily staying at The Noel Hotel until I find a place. By the way, would you know of any rooms that are for rent?"

"Not at the moment, but I'll ask around and let you know," Sadie answered.

Smiling as she left the boutique, Louise was excited about her good fortune of meeting a new friend. She stepped outside into the warmth and brightness of the morning sun.

Louise was looking forward to having dinner with Calvin and learning more about his life. There was something about his worldliness that intrigued her. *I wish I could buy him a small gift to show my appreciation for his generosity,* Louise thought. Noticing an interesting-looking antique shop across the street, she opened the heavy, gilded door and stepped inside. An opulent pair of gold-leaved Nubian statues ornamented the vestibule. Black and white marble tiles graced the floor with an eight-pointed star pattern. Patchouli incense was slowly burning on the counter wafting its fragrant aroma throughout the space. Louise was astonished as she admired the fine pieces of period furniture, lamps, and decorative accessories. She wondered, *What is the story of these valuable possessions and the people who owned them?*

As she walked to the jewelry counter, the owner introduced herself. "Hello! I'm Tara, may I help you?"

"Yes, thanks. I'm hoping to find a gift for a gentleman, but I don't have much money to spend."

Tara scanned the glass display cabinets. "Perhaps I have the perfect gift for you at a great price. Look at these Ying Yang cufflinks made of ebony and ivory set in sterling silver. They are originally from Paris and were made in the early 1800s. I can't sell them for what they're worth because there's a chip on the underside of one. Personally, I think that adds to their character. They're antique, after all."

Louise replied, "I love the symbolic meaning. They're the perfect gift. I'll take them." Louise was consciously aware of her money, but considering what Calvin had done for her, she thought they would be a nice gesture to show her appreciation. After agreeing on a price, Tara polished the silver and placed the cufflinks, along with a brief description, into an attractive box. She then gift-wrapped them with white tissue paper and cobalt blue ribbon.

Louise decided to spend the rest of the day exploring Nashville. She walked a few blocks down to the Cumberland River and gazed at a paddle-wheel boat chugging up the river. Excitement flooded her soul. She really loved the vibrant city and how different it was from New River Gorge.

Cumulus clouds drifted lazily through the immense blue sky. Although the day was rather warm, a nice cool breeze blew from the river. Inspired by her surroundings, Louise sat down on a park bench under a shady oak tree and watched a brilliant Eastern Bluebird warble its cheerful song. As she took a journal from her purse, her thoughts were immediately on Hank. He haunted her dreams, and she missed him more each passing day. She worried about his safety and wondered how he was coping with the pain of her desertion.

Filled with emotions, Louise began writing a song. *I left Nowhere with hope that you would come find me, my dear. Can't you hear my heart calling your name? Come find me, my darling, in a place that's beyond heartache and fear. Can't you hear my heart calling your name?*

Louise glanced at the clock on the bank tower and was surprised at how late it was. As she strolled back to the hotel, a well-dressed couple passed her on the sidewalk. The gentleman tipped his hat, and the lady gave a genuine smile. The friendliness of strangers on the streets pleasantly surprised her.

Everyone she had met possessed a positive energy that encouraged her to believe that she was on the right path.

✤

The elegant Birdcage Lounge at The Noel Hotel was crowded with well-dressed businessmen and elaborately dressed women. A constant buzz of conversation and laughter rose above the music provided by a jazz pianist. Louise walked into the bar feeling insecure, although she looked stunning in her newly-acquired black dress.

"Oh, my! Louise, you look divine," Calvin said as he approached her. "Come, let's sit at the bar and have a Sazerac. It's my favorite New Orleans cocktail."

"Sure, that's a delicious-sounding name for a cocktail," Louise said as they claimed two bar stools.

Calvin signaled to Nick, the bartender, and ordered two Sazeracs. Louise watched as he placed four chilled old-fashion glasses on the bar. Nick swirled a wash of Absinthe into two of them. Then he combined a shot of cognac brandy, rye whiskey, bitters, and a cube of sugar in the other two glasses. Adding ice, he stirred and strained the mixture into the glasses containing the Absinthe, serving them without delay. Nick said cheerfully, "Laissez les bon temps rouler. [Let the good times roll.]"

Raising his glass, Calvin proposed a toast: "Cheers, Louise. It's an honor to have met you. May the clouds in your life be only a background for a lovely sunset."

Louise paused and returned a toast of her own: "Calvin, the honor is mine. Here's to letting go of the past, trusting in the future, and rejoicing in the glorious now." Louise took a sip of her cocktail and was surprised at the sweet, spicy, and herbal flavors.

"Great sentiment; now tell me about your day."

Reaching into her bag, Louise retrieved the gift and presented it to Calvin. "I have a small token of appreciation for the kindness you have shown me," she said.

When he opened the present, his eyes lit up showing that he absolutely loved the antique cuff links. For a man rarely without words, Calvin was deeply touched and for a moment could only manage a smile. "Louise, thank you. What a thoughtful gift! I will treasure them always."

After finishing their drinks, they were promptly seated in the dining room and the waiter approached. Calvin wasted no time ordering two more Sazeracs. He wanted to savor every moment of the evening. Louise intrigued Calvin. She had stirred within him a paternal sentimentality wherefore he felt protective of her. He loosened his tie, looked at her admiringly, and thought, Somehow, *I believe that meeting Louise on the train was kismet and definitely not happenstance.*

CHAPTER 11

Seductive Green Eyes

$\mathcal{H}$ank received his engineer's certification on a Friday afternoon and accepted an invitation from a few co-workers to celebrate with a couple of beers. They walked into The Yard Arm Tavern and grabbed a stool at the old, wooden bar. Hank was damn proud of himself, but he genuinely wished that Charlie could have been there to enjoy the moment. After several rounds of the house draft, Hank said, "Boys, as much as I would like to keep this party going, I've got to go finish the railing on Tallulah's steps." At the mention of her name, his buddies whistled and applauded. It seemed that she had been the subject of all their imaginations. Hank laughed, "Trust me—ain't nothing going on there."

While leaving the bar, Hank noticed the wind had picked up and the sky had turned dark. He hitched a ride to the carriage house. By the time he got out of the car, a saturating rain was falling, causing him to run. He stripped out of his wet clothes and took a hot shower. Leaving the front door open for the cool breeze, he could hear the sounds of water cascading off the roof. Until that moment, he had never understood why Louise loved the rain so much. A slow, soaking rain gently fell refreshing the atmosphere. *Looks like it's going to be an all-nighter. No repairs on the house today,* Hank thought. Too much celebrating had made him sleepy, so he laid his wet head on the soft, down pillows and passed out.

About an hour later a soft knock awakened him. Grabbing the towel he had dropped beside the bed, he wrapped it around himself and drowsily made his way to the door. There stood Tallulah underneath an umbrella. "I'm sorry, Hank. Am I disturbing you?"

"No. Please come in," he stammered.

"Actually, I came to invite you for dinner to celebrate your certification. I've cooked spaghetti and meatballs."

"Thanks, that would be great. Just give me a couple minutes and I'll be right over."

When Hank walked into her house, the divine smell of homemade marinara made his stomach rumble with anticipation. Breathing in the aroma of the Italian dish, Hank commented, "Tallulah, this is really nice. Thank you. Can I do anything to help?"

"No, thanks, just have a seat." She gestured towards a beautifully set table and two chairs perfectly placed within an architectural niche. Lovely Peonies graced a simple vase and two candles lit the table. Hank sat down and felt a nice breeze blowing through the open windows. The rain was still falling softly. Johnny Mercer's "Lazy Bones" was playing on the Gramophone.

Hank started singing along: "Lazy bones, sleepin' in the sun, how you 'spect to get your day's work done?"

"Nice voice," Tallulah teased.

Hank chuckled and replied, "Aw! Thanks! I don't think I'm any good, but I do enjoy singing when I play my guitar or listen to music."

"Actually, you sound pretty good to me. I found a drink recipe in a magazine that also sounds good," Tallulah announced. "It's a New Orleans cocktail called a Sazerac, and I decided to try it out on you. It was difficult to find all the ingredients, but I hope you like it." Handing Hank a drink, she raised her glass. "Cheers! Congratulations! You're a great guy and deserve this opportunity."

"Thank you, Tallulah. I appreciate your cooking this fine meal. I wish Charlie were here to enjoy it with us." Hank took a sip of his drink and was amazed. He had never tasted anything so exotic.

Tallulah placed dinner on the table. Hank was ravenous and unapologetically went for a second helping while mumbling that the spaghetti and meatballs were the best he had ever tasted. He froze for a moment when he glanced up and noticed Tallulah's smile. Candlelight was dancing off her seductive, green eyes, and he had to look away from her raw beauty.

Noticing his discomfort, she said, "These dishes can wait. Come, let's go into the living room and talk. I want to hear all of your story, Hank." She grabbed two glasses and a bottle of Jack Daniel's. "That fancy drink was nice, but let's have some smooth Tennessee whiskey. Shall we?"

"Tallulah, I like your style," Hank teased while following her to the sofa.

Enjoying their whiskey, they both relaxed and candidly shared their stories. Conversation flowed naturally—creating a relationship of trust. The storm suddenly increased in intensity, and rain beat down hard on the slate roof. Strong, gusty winds rushed through the swaying trees. Lightning flashed viciously illuminating the dark sky. Thunder boomed loudly in response jarring the windows. The atmosphere seemed charged with electricity. Just as Tallulah decided to light more candles, lightning struck somewhere close by knocking out the electricity. Queenie ran and hid beneath the bed. They looked at each other for a serious moment, and then burst out laughing.

When their humor had subsided, Hank stood up to leave. "Tallulah, thank you for this special evening. This has been really nice but I don't want to overstay my welcome."

She grabbed him gently by his arm. "Hank, you can't go out in this weather right now. Please, sit back down. I want to tell you something." She held his hand and looked directly into his blue eyes. "I know you're hurting inside and missing Louise. I understand that kind of pain and loneliness that comes from being the one who was left behind. Through no fault of his own, my husband died and left me behind. You and I are both wounded and lonely people totally in need of affection, and there's nothing wrong with that. I know you love Louise, and I sincerely hope that you find her; but tonight I'm the one in need of your touch." She leaned over and gently kissed his lips. His body responded to her touch immediately in a way that surprised him. Hank's neglected needs overruled his senses. Whatever will-power he had possessed immediately deserted him.

Without hesitation she led Hank into the bedroom. He unbuttoned her dress, and when it slipped off her voluptuous body, he hastily removed his own clothing. He gazed upon Tallulah and desire filled him. They kissed in desperate longing. Hank carried her to the bed. His mouth continued kissing her all over. He ran his fingers through her thick, silky hair, tenderly brushing it away from her face. Gently stroking the sensual curve of her neck, Hank held her in a tender embrace.

Tallulah heard a moan and recognized it as her own. She forgot about everything in that moment except the kiss. She felt her body melt into that sensation.

Hank filled his hands with the ripeness of her lovely breasts and gently touched each nipple. Then he kissed her again more passionately and caressed the warm flesh between her thighs. Hank was so aroused that his hunger could not be denied another second. Their pelvises were grinding together in unison while making love in exquisite slow-motion. There was a mutual healing happening as their bodies pleasured each other with their sweet love-making.

When they were both spent, he pulled her closer and they drifted into a deep sleep. It seemed the storm had also expired along with the expenditure of their energy.

CHAPTER 12

Guardian Angel

*L*ouise was feeling flushed from the Sazerac cocktails. Excusing herself, she made for the ladies room to freshen up. Glancing in the bathroom mirror, she was surprised to see the image of the person she had become staring back at her. A queasy feeling swept over her, and she held onto the sink for stability. Her hazel eyes misted over, exposing her vulnerability. She missed Hank so much that the ache in her heart seemed unnatural. Louise thought, *What am I doing? Hank, how can I go on without you? I've got to pull myself together.* She splashed cold water on her face and gently blotted it dry. Taking a couple of deep breaths, she steadied herself to return to Calvin. As Louise crossed the room, she noticed a well-dressed gentleman speaking with Calvin. When she approached the table, they both stood. Calvin made the introductions. "Louise, please allow me to introduce Mr. Cody Withers, general manager of The Noel Hotel."

"So nice to meet you, Mr. Withers. Please take a seat," Louise said while offering her hand.

"Nice to meet you, Louise. Please just call me Cody. Calvin was explaining that you've recently arrived in Nashville and you're looking to find a start in the music industry. What style music do you sing, and do you play an instrument?"

Louise took a sip of ice water and confidently said, "I can sing a variety of styles, but my favorite is blues and jazz. I've been working on a rendition of 'Sweet Home Chicago' that I really enjoy. My instrument is the fiddle or violin, depending on which way it's played."

"Splendid! Louise, I'm currently holding auditions for a new entertainer for The Birdcage Lounge. Would you be willing to come to my office at nine in the morning for an audition?"

Without hesitation she responded: "Yes, Cody, I definitely would be. Thanks for offering me a chance. I look forward to seeing you in the morning."

"Very well, I'll see you then. In the meantime, I have business to take care of, so you two enjoy your dinner. Calvin, let's talk soon. I want to hear more about your Costa Rican adventures.

After Cody left, Calvin said, "Opportunity is already knocking at your door, my lady."

"And it's all because of you. Thank you, Calvin. I will always be grateful," Louise replied.

The waiter presented their dinner of roasted duck with an orange glaze. The duck was sitting atop a wild rice medley with a side of candied yams. Using constraint, she kept herself from devouring the meal right in front of Calvin. Louise was beyond hungry. Compared to the humble food she was used to preparing, this dinner was delectable.

After finishing her last, delicious bite, Louise praised the chef and then said to Calvin, "Now please tell me all about Costa Rica."

Calvin responded, "Yes, that duck was roasted perfectly. I'm glad you enjoyed it, and I love to see a woman with an appetite. Well, a few years back I took a trip to Costa Rica to check out whether importing their coffee would be profitable. I fell in love with the country and purchased a working coffee plantation. There's something so flavorful and aromatic about coffee grown under the Central American skies. It has a hint of floral and fruitiness somewhat like Hibiscus or Pomegranate. My beans were soon in high demand, so I became a coffee distributor for fine establishments across the country, including The Noel Hotel and Maxwell House here in Nashville. I guess you could sum up my success as simply being in the right place at the right time, or just dumb luck."

"You're being modest. I'm sure there was more to it than luck. Please tell me about the country itself," Louise said.

Calvin chuckled and replied, "Ahh! Costa Rica! How does one explain such beauty and complexity? Costa Rica is a lush tropical rainforest where, of the whole Central American coastline, the mountains come the closest to the Pacific Ocean. The temperate climate and ocean breezes make for an ideal place to live. The native people are called Ticos and are mostly a very peaceful and friendly people. Delicious fruits such as papayas, mangoes, and pineapples grow naturally. Every evening, fishermen bring in their fresh catch of fish, shrimp and lobster. Life illustrates itself everywhere through color, scent and sound." Calvin took a drink and paused before continuing. "I haven't even mentioned the abundance of exotic birds and wildlife. Palm trees line beautiful sandy beaches where a mighty surf roars in. My coffee plantation, Finca La Puerta del Alma, [The Gateway of the Soul] is in the higher elevations where the temperature is ideal for growing perfect coffee beans. I could talk about this all night because Costa Rica is in my soul. It has its challenges, no doubt, but I love it there. Now it's your turn. Please tell me your story of how you came to be in Nashville."

Louise was feeling relaxed and very content with a full stomach. "Well, my story certainly isn't that interesting or exciting, but I'll share." Louise told him about the fire that took her family and how she had left Hank and hocked her grandmother's ring to come to Nashville. She continued, "Like many others, I'm just another country girl who's trying to make it in a big city."

Calvin was touched by her story. He said, "Darling, there's no other like you, trust me. I have the utmost respect for your courage. You've had to make some very difficult choices, but I believe your sacrifice will be worth it. Don't ever give up on your dreams."

Calvin looked at his pocket watch. Noticing the time, he said, "Oh! My dear, I'm sorry I've kept you so late. I have so enjoyed our time together, and I sincerely thank you for sharing your story. I'm afraid I must say 'goodnight,' as I'm catching the early morning train back to New Orleans. Louise, I sincerely wish you all the best. Good luck with your audition, and don't forget to go see Sonny at the recording studio. I look forward to seeing you perform on my next trip to Nashville."

"I can't thank you enough for everything you've done for me, Calvin. You have been my guardian angel. I look forward to your return visit and hearing more of your Costa Rican adventures. Until our paths cross again, I wish you a safe journey."

Taking her hand, Calvin gently kissed it. "You are a special lady, Louise, and you deserve the best. May I escort you to your room?"

Louise gave him a tender look and replied, "Yes, you may."

At her door, Calvin kissed her on the cheek and said goodnight and farewell. He walked towards the elevator thinking, *There's something exceptional about Louise. Her courage makes me optimistic for America's future.*

CHAPTER 13

Tangled Web

*H*ank teetered on the fringe of consciousness as the fragile dawn before sunrise gradually lightened the night sky. A gentle breeze, cooled by the night's rain, blew through the open window. He reached for the tangled covers to combat the morning chill. Hank had slept fitfully. He dreamed of floating deeper and deeper into the cold and wet mine until he was absorbed into the grim nothingness. Queenie sat beside the bed and affectionately licked his hand, causing Hank to emerge from his nightmare. He slowly opened his eyes to the awkward reality that he was lying in bed with another woman. He inhaled a big gasp of air and exhaled slowly. Hank could not help but be aroused as he admired Tallulah's naked body next to his. Guilt came screaming through his confused mind. He thought, *My God, what have I done?*

Trying not to wake Tallulah, Hank slipped silently out of bed. Fortunately, she moaned and rolled over still sleeping. He got dressed and decided to take Queenie for an early morning jog. Hank thought, *I could use some fresh air and a long run to clear my head.* Hank left the house with Queenie and started running with extra vigor down Franklin Road.

Tallulah stretched and slowly opened her eyes, noticing that Hank and Queenie were gone. She felt grateful because too much whiskey had caused her to inherit a rough morning. Tallulah felt bad, and the feeling was more apparent when she saw her image reflected in the mirror. As she brushed her teeth, snapshots of the night before flashed through her mind. The recollections of their love-making made her skin tingle. Dressing quickly she headed to the kitchen to prepare a hearty breakfast to help relieve her hangover.

Tallulah heard the back door open and Queenie came running to her. She called to Hank, but he did not answer. Glancing out the window, she saw him walking towards the carriage house. She thought, *I guess he's feeling a little awkward too. It's best to leave him alone for a while. If only things were different, I could fall for Hank, but clearly Louise is the one who has his heart.*

Even though it was Hank's day off, he decided to hitch a ride down to the station and see if he could up pick an extra shift. He thought, *I need to get away from Tallulah— coward that I am. I can't face her after last night. Truth be told, I'm afraid of that woman. It would be easy to fall for her, and that just can't happen. I've got to find Louise and the sooner the better.*

Hank walked into the trainmaster's office, and Mr. Johnson looked up from his desk, "Good morning, Hank. I thought this was your day off."

"Good morning, Mr. Johnson. It is my day off, sir. I'm just checking to see if there's any extra work."

Mr. Johnson responded, "I've got an engine that's broken down in Birmingham, and I could use an extra set of hands to get her back. It would be an overnighter, but you'd get paid time and a half. Are you interested?"

Hank answered, "Yes sir. Thank you. I'd be happy to help out. When do I leave?"

Mr. Johnson replied, "Right now. Get your things. Take locomotive number thirteen. It has the most power but go easy on that throttle."

Charlie came home exhausted from his Chattanooga trip. He gave his sister a big hug and said, "Where's Hank?"

Tallulah answered, "I'm not sure."

On his way to the shower, Charlie grabbed a piece of bacon and said, "It's been a long night. I've gotta get some sleep."

When Charlie awoke from his nap, Tallulah expressed her concern about Hank. It wasn't like him to leave without telling anyone where he was going. Charlie couldn't find Hank either so he called the yard to learn if anyone there had seen him. A flagman affectionately called "Ole Red" informed him that Hank had picked up an extra turn and wouldn't be back until the next afternoon.

Tallulah was relieved when Charlie shared the news about Hank. They needed some space to let their feelings pass.

"I'm going out with a friend tonight, so don't wait up. What if I cook dinner tomorrow night, and we can catch up with Hank? He's really missed you," Tallulah said.

"Sis, that sounds like an awesome idea. I'll find out what time he's expected in and I'll pick him up at the yard. Damn, it's good to be back home, and I've got three days before I have to leave again. Any news regarding Louise?"

Tallulah sighed and said, "As far as Louise, I haven't heard any news." She felt a stab of guilt, and Sir Walter Scott's quote came to mind, "Oh! What a tangled web we weave, when first we practice to deceive."

CHAPTER 14

Fate Be Kind

Louise lay in her dark room trying to diminish the self-sabotaging thoughts that consumed her. She arose at the break of dawn to prepare for her audition, but anxiety washed over her like a giant wave eroding her confidence. *What made me think I could pull this off? If I don't get this audition what's going to happen to me?*

Grandmother Octavia had encouraged Louise to let go of paralyzing fear and shift her attention and energy towards a positive outcome. Remembering this, Louise stopped fretting and did her breathing exercises, followed by her favorite affirmations. *"I have the power to convert my fear into positive energy and manifest my dreams. I radiate confidence. I believe in myself."*

Cody met Louise at the door and ushered her into the conference room. "Good morning. Hope you're feeling well. I'm on a tight schedule, so thanks for being prompt. I have set up the mic, so whenever you're ready, you may begin."

Louise shook off any remaining feelings of insecurity. She wanted and needed this job badly. Knowing that this was her big chance, she confidently stepped up to the mic and began to sing acapella. Her voice resonated strong and true as she maintained the rhythm and tempo. She sang a standard and one of her original pieces accompanied by her instrument.

Cody listened intently. Without showing any emotion, he took a sip of water and paused as though he were trying to make a difficult decision. The silence was intimidating as Louise was uncertain of what he was thinking. *Fate be kind. This is a make it or break it moment,* Louise thought.

Finally, Cody looked at her passively. "Louise, you have an interesting texture to your voice with an impressive range. You also have the ability to sing the darker and lower octaves. Your voice is perfectly suited for singing blues and jazz, as well as country music. With an orchestra accompanying you, I'm certain any audience would adore you." Without fanfare Cody announced. "Louise, the job is yours. Actually, you have saved me from a predicament. My last entertainer left Nashville suddenly, and I've been searching for a replacement. Your first performance will be Saturday night at 8:00 p.m. I apologize for such short notice."

Louise gasped. She could hardly believe it. With a delighted look, she replied, "Cody, thank you for this wonderful opportunity. I promise not to let you down."

Cody presented a contract and they went over it line by line. "Please find in the envelope a cash advance. Your room and meals at The Noel are also included in your compensation. If everything is to your satisfaction, please sign and date here. I need for you to meet with the orchestra at two this afternoon for rehearsal, and I'll have my photographer there to get a nice headshot. Louise, if there's any advice I can give you, it's just be your natural self. Don't let stage fright paralyze you. If you'll excuse me, I need to promote your first appearance by submitting a press release. Congratulations, Louise, you're going to be a wonderful addition to The Noel Hotel."

While walking out of Cody's office, Louise reflected on something Calvin had said to her on the train: "Imagine this. Dreams offer an image of a future that you desire. They energize your mind and impel you forward. Dreams fill you with empowering emotions. Inspiration is everywhere, but it's your will that keeps dreams alive." Louise embraced the moment. *All the sacrifices I've made to get here are beginning to pay off.*

Louise's initial rehearsal with the Big Band Swing & Jazz Orchestra went flawlessly due to their talent and professionalism. Although she had listened to the Grand Ole Opry since she was young, the new tempo and rhythm of swing and jazz resonated with her in an energizing way. This uplifting music blended contrasting moods of the Great Depression with the glamorous movies of Hollywood. With Louise's musical gift and natural talent, she was a quick study. The band loved her instinctive presence on the stage.

Billboard Magazine's weekly publication, *Hit Parade,* showcased the most popular songs of the time. Louise's repertoire for her musical revue included a few of those songs such as: "Farewell Blues," "Darktown Strutters Ball" and "Sailor Man Rhythm."

Louise left the rehearsal feeling elated. She went immediately to share the good news with Sadie. Thanks to Cody's cash advance, she was now in the position to buy a chic new gown and accessories for her debut.

"Hey, girl. How are you doing?" Sadie greeted Louise as she strolled into the boutique. "I was just thinking of leaving you a note at the hotel. Would you like to get together Saturday evening?"

"I have an even better idea," Louise said, all excited. "I got the job at The Birdcage Lounge. I'll be singing there Saturday night, and I'd like for you to come as my guest. It would be great to see a familiar face in the audience."

"Oh, my God, how exciting! Louise, I'm so happy for you."

"Thanks, I can hardly believe it myself. Sadie, I need to ask you a favor. Would you please style my hair and apply makeup for the show? I haven't a clue how to do that."

"Yes, silly! Of course I will. What if I come to your room about five o'clock on Saturday?"

"That would be great! In the meantime, I need an exquisite gown and a new pair of classy shoes," Louise answered.

"I just displayed the most gorgeous backless gown. It's emerald-green velvet trimmed with rhinestones around the neckline, and it comes with a beautiful satin-lined cape with fur trim. I thought of you the moment I saw it. Come look at this beauty."

"Sadie, you're right. It's perfect." Louise was astonished at how well it fit. The velvet clung to her body, and a cascade of silk fabric fell below her knees. Louise wanted to make a statement at her opening, and this gown would definitely accomplish that.

Louise met with the orchestra for her final rehearsal. She could hardly wait to perform with them before a live audience. Upon returning to her room, she opened the door to find two dozen long-stemmed yellow roses in a gorgeous vase. The card read: *Knock 'em dead, Louise. Wish I could be there for your big night. With Love, Calvin.*

At 5:00 p.m. sharp Sadie arrived eager to help prepare Louise for her big night. Retrieving her flask, she said, "Louise, let's have a little sip of whiskey to calm our nerves and to celebrate your big night before we get started."

Sadie trimmed Louise's hair and styled it in a side-swept chignon leaving a few strands falling free to frame her face. She applied eye shadow and mascara with a touch of rouge and a deep red lipstick. Louise looked ravishing and was finally ready for her big night.

When the elevator opened into the lobby, they were taken aback at the large crowd that had gathered. Cody met Louise to escort her backstage, while Sadie was ushered to her reserved seat at a front table. Tension was building as the audience in The Birdcage Lounge anticipated Louise O'Neill's opening night.

CHAPTER 15

Soulful Voice

$\mathcal{H}$ank arrived at Union Station with the damaged locomotive in tow. He was feeling a little bleary until he saw Charlie waiting for him. They gave each other big hugs and slaps on the back.

"Hank, man, it's good to see you. How was your run to Birmingham?"

Hank took off his engineer's hat and stuck it in his back pocket. "It was an opportunity to pick up some overtime and more experience. It's great to see you too, Charlie. It's been awfully quiet without you."

They checked in with the office, and Mr. Johnson said, "Hank, there's a note for you pinned to the corkboard."

"Thanks." Hank retrieved the note and read aloud:

Hank, there's a bill posted at The Noel Hotel announcing that Louise O'Neill is making her singing debut Saturday night at eight o'clock in The Birdcage Lounge.

Good luck, Joe.

His heart raced and his hand trembled as he thought, *Can this be real? Have my prayers been answered?*

"Hank, this is your big break! Congratulations, I told you we'd find her," Charlie said.

On the ride home Hank was thinking about Tallulah and how they were going to handle seeing one another again. Charlie pulled into the driveway

73   **TRACKS FROM NOWHERE**

sooner than Hank expected. When he noticed Tallulah and Queenie on the porch to greet them, it only added to his sense of uneasiness.

"Welcome back. I'm glad you're home safely. Supper is at six. Hope you have an appetite because I've made a big pot of venison chili and jalapeno cornbread," Tallulah announced.

Hank felt relieved by her relaxed manner. "I'm really happy to be back, and I have exciting news to share." He handed her the card regarding Louise.

"Hank, this is fantastic news! I'm so happy for you. We must go see her perform tonight."

Hank thought, *What a gal to be so unselfish and caring!*

The pleasant fall weather was starting to wane, but the flaming trees were still showing off some of their vivid colors. Fall had always been Hank and Louise's favorite time of year. While touching the note in his pocket he longed for her. With the time that had passed between them, Hank was wondering how it would feel to hold her in his arms again. A subtle thrill of excitement coursed through him at the thought of watching her perform on stage.

Silence prevailed as they enjoyed the spicy chili. There seemed to be a sense of shared relief to think that the search for Louise could be over. Yet, each in their own way were also wondering how this news was going to change things.

After supper, Tallulah brought out a bottle of whiskey along with glasses. She poured three fingers of Jack Daniel's in each. A cool evening breeze was blowing through the open screened windows—teasing the candle flame.

Charlie raised his glass. "Here's to our good friend Hank. Congratulations! We're thrilled to have you on our team at the rails: but more importantly, congrats on finding Louise. Now you've got to win her back."

"Thanks for helping a poor old coal miner out of a bad situation. Y'all mean a lot to me. Cheers! And yes, I can hardly wait to see Louise again."

Hank, Charlie and Tallulah entered The Birdcage Lounge and took notice of the ambiance of the spacious room. The opulence of the space was unlike anything Hank had ever seen. Tallulah approached the hostess and asked for a table for three. The hostess apologized and informed them that there was only one table left, and it was in the back-left corner.

Tallulah quickly replied, "Thanks, we'll take it."

Hank stepped up and insisted on paying the cover charge, then the hostess escorted them to their table. Once drinks were in hand, they raised their glasses in unison. "Here's to finding Louise."

The curtain parted slowly, and there stood Louise looking amazing in an elegant, green, velvet gown. She stood gracefully beside a Baby Grand Piano with an ensemble of musicians behind her. The stage lights gradually came up, accenting her beauty even more. Hank was speechless and his hands began to tremble slightly. He was so nervous and could hardly believe what he was seeing. Pride for Louise swelled in his heart. *Could this possibly be my wife? The same woman who endured such a humble existence is now standing on this stage looking like a star. Louise, darling, you're realizing your dream.*

While Hank was in dialogue with himself, Louise started to sing in the most melodic voice ever. Charlie punched Hank on the arm and said, "Man, is that really her?"

Hank was inarticulate and simply nodded his head.

Tallulah was sitting there also looking stunned. She thought, *No wonder Hank is madly in love with Louise. She's amazingly beautiful and has such a soulful voice.*

Louise's final song of the evening was an Irish love song called "Grace." She explained, "This song is about Grace Gifford and Joseph Plunkett. They were only married for fifteen short minutes before Joseph's execution in 1916 at Kilmainham Prison. He was executed for participating in the rising of Dublin, Ireland. Grace's love for Joseph lives on in this song."

His eyes watered, but Hank didn't care how he looked. When Louise sang that haunting love song, it always brought him to his knees. She finished the song strong and took a bow. Hank realized that Louise was receiving a standing ovation. He was laughing and crying at the same time. Before walking off stage, she blew a kiss to the crowd and Hank secretly wished it was for him.

After the crowd settled down, Hank prepared to make his move. Then he saw a handsome, well-dressed gentleman approach Louise and kiss the back of her gloved hand. They talked for a few minutes, and then he escorted her to a table by the stage. The man kept his hand on hers while they laughed and talked. Several other gentlemen approached her table and were congratulating her as well. A bucket of champagne with two glasses and a box of roses were delivered to the table. Louise was laughing and having the time of her life. Reality hit Hank like a brick, *She's going to become a star. How can I ever stand in her way? The best thing I can do is leave, so I won't embarrass her. She's already moved on. I've lost her.*

Hank walked deliberately through the crowded room and out the front door feeling deflated, like the very breath of life had been knocked out of him. Charlie and Tallulah immediately followed.

When they arrived at the house, Hank went straight to his room so he could be alone to drink and brood. He felt about as low as a man could get. About an hour later, there was a light knock at the door. Hank gruffly said, "Go away! I'm not good company tonight."

Tallulah opened the door and went in—regardless. She sat down on the sofa beside him and said, "Hank, look at me. You've found Louise; now fight for her. Don't look so defeated. Get your head out of the clouds and pick your heart up off the floor. Instead of brooding, start thinking of how to win her back; because, Hank, if you don't, you're going to regret it the rest of your days."

"Can't you see I've lost her already? She's going to be a big star. I blew my chance with her."

Tallulah gently took his hand and said, "If you truly believe that, then it is so. Hank, you do not remind me of the kind of man who would just roll over so easily and give up on someone you love."

Hank took another swig of whiskey and said, "Tallulah, I owe you the biggest apology ever. Please forgive me for walking out on you the other morning. I'm really sorry. That was cowardly of me. You're one of the most amazing women I've ever met. Truth be told, I was intimidated by my feelings for you. Instead of talking with you, I ran away and I do regret that." Hank paused for reflection. "Tallulah, you're right. Somehow I've got to see Louise and find out if she still has feelings for me."

Tallulah arose from the sofa and kissed him softly on the lips. "Now that's the Hank I know. Please, you do not owe me any apology or explanation. What we shared was simply a sweet moment in time when we both needed each other. Having guilt would only dishonor that." Tallulah said goodnight. As she left him, the screen door slammed gently behind her.

CHAPTER 16

Unrivaled Talent

Louise stood beside the Baby Grand awaiting her introduction. She heard Cody pick up the mic as the stage curtain parted. "Good evening, everyone. Thanks for coming out tonight. We have a special treat for your listening pleasure. Once you hear her sing, you will agree that she is headed for stardom. Remember, you heard her first here at The Birdcage Lounge. Ladies and gentlemen, without further ado, I give you Louise O'Neill."

Stepping up to the mic, Louise bowed to her audience and politely thanked everyone for coming. She started the set with "Farewell Blues." As she sang, Louise felt lifted above any stage fright. The romantic song seemed to come straight from her soul. She glided effortlessly across the stage and glanced into the audience and found Sadie's reassuring smile. The orchestra was excellent, and they flowed totally in sync with Louise throughout the production. She performed some lively jazz tunes, but the haunting love song "Grace" was her final number. It was Hank's favorite. Louise picked up her fiddle, and smiling at the audience, she gracefully drew the bow across the strings. The heart-piercing tone resonated throughout the room. With a strong finale, she brought down the house. Everyone was standing, clapping and cheering loudly. Louise realized she was receiving a standing ovation. She bowed to her adoring audience and wished that Hank could have seen her in this amazing moment. Louise blew a kiss, but in her heart it was meant for Hank.

Louise stepped down from the stage and a good-looking man more than six-feet tall with sandy blond hair and blue eyes approached her. He was a sharp-dressed man sporting a windowpane sport coat, a blue satin vest, grey pants, and a red scarf. His larger-than-life appearance spoke of his confidence and optimism. He smiled, took her hand and kissed it, "Hello, Louise. Please allow me to introduce myself. My name is Sonny Reinheart. I'm a music producer and agent. Your performance tonight was captivating. I have a company called Sound Production Studio, and I would like to talk with you about a recording contract. I think with a little experience, you have the potential to become a star. Would you please be so kind as to join me at my table?"

"Certainly. That sounds lovely." *Is it possible that this could be the Sonny Reinheart that Calvin told me about?* Sonny escorted her to his table and ordered a bottle of expensive champagne. Louise sat down and felt inside her small purse, pulled out a card, and handed it to Sonny. "You're Calvin's friend, right?"

Sonny looked surprised and said, "Wow! If this isn't fate. You'll have to share the story of how you know Calvin. He's a great guy, that one."

Suddenly she was surrounded by a throne of men congratulating her. She was feeling a bit overwhelmed when she looked up and saw Sadie watching and motioned for her to come over. Sadie joined them at the table. The chilled champagne was delivered along with a dozen red roses compliments of The Noel Hotel.

Raising his glass, Sonny said, "Cheers! Here's to you, Louise. You are going places, and I would love to be the one to take you there."

After the champagne, Sonny asked, "May I have the honor of taking you two ladies out for a late dinner? I know a fine intimate restaurant called The Brass Rail where we can talk and relax. They are well-known for their steaks, and their seafood is excellent."

Louise looked delighted and replied, "Thanks, Sonny. That would be wonderful."

After dinner, Sonny asked, "Louise, would you meet me at my office in the morning at ten o'clock so we can discuss your career plans? I'll send a car to pick you up."

"Certainly, I look forward to it," Louise answered.

Standing outside the restaurant, Sonny was looking intently at Louise like he had something important to say, yet he seemed to hesitate.

Sadie picked up on the moment and said, "I live just around the corner, so I'm going to walk home. Goodnight, and thanks again for dinner. Louise, I'll talk with you tomorrow."

Sonny smiled and asked. "It's such a lovely night for a walk. May I escort you back to the hotel?"

"Yes, thank you," Louise answered appreciatively.

Sonny was curious. "Louise, have you written any original songs?"

"Yes. Actually I've written several. The latest I'm working on is called 'Tracks From Nowhere.' It sort of resembles my life as of late." They arrived at the hotel. "Good night, Sonny. It was nice to have met you and thanks again for dinner."

"It was my pleasure. I look forward to seeing you tomorrow morning. Good night, Louise."

With a little pep in his step, Sonny walked down the street whistling "I've Got Rhythm" and thinking, *When Louise sang that song tonight, I knew that she was unrivaled in talent.*

CHAPTER 17

Ghost Riders

*H*ank and Charlie were at the station early Monday morning viewing the schedule board for their weekly assignments when Mr. Johnson walked in. "Good morning, boys. You won't find your names on the board today. I need the two of you to dead-head an engine to Fayetteville. We need more horsepower to pull the extra one-hundred-ton coal hoppers added to the train So get moving."

I'm glad to have the opportunity to work with Charlie. He's much more seasoned and I can gain some valuable experience, Hank thought. They fired up the engine and did the safety precautions checklist. With a sharp hiss from the release of the air brakes, they were on their way.

When the train was rolling down the rails, Charlie looked at Hank and said, "Man, are you ok? Louise is an amazing talent. Seeing her last night must have been really intense."

"Yep, that was intense to say the least. I still haven't figured out how I'm going to deal with our situation. After we return, I've got to find a way to talk with her. I never thought she would have the courage to leave me and go it alone. Boy, did I ever underestimate that woman! Louise has too much talent to remain in a place like New River Gorge. There's no opportunity there for anyone to advance. I've never blamed her, in fact, I admire and respect her tenacity." Hank went into more detail about the promise he had made to his father on his deathbed—the vow that trapped him and Louise into a life of unfulfilled dreams. "If only I could go back in time. Unfortunately, life is not lived in hindsight. I'm sorry, Charlie. I'm rambling."

Letting the conversation drop for a while, Charlie then said, "Hank, that was a tough predicament that you were in. You're an honorable man; and although it wasn't wise, you did what you thought was right. No one can blame you for that."

Charlie checked the gauges and after a few minutes asked, "So, whatever happened with your mother?"

"She went to live with her sister in Fayetteville." Hank took a deep sigh and resumed. "My mother never cared much for Louise; she would always find fault and criticize her. Louise was gracious, but it was never enough to appease Mother. She has an abusive tongue and doesn't mind using it. Sarcasm follows her like a toxic rain cloud. I guess it comes from living a hard life and having proud Irish blood that accounts for her bitterness."

"Hank, you've got to find a way to talk with Louise. Don't automatically assume that she doesn't want you anymore. You shouldn't let the fact that she's star-bound intimidate you. I'm sure she still loves you. You can't just stop loving someone because it's convenient. The only advice I have for you is to think things through with your head and not just your heart. When you react with emotions, things tend to get heated."

Charlie opened the window to let in some fresh air then checked the gauges. All was well. The chugging sound of the escaping steam and the rhythmic clickity-clack of the wheels moving over the tracks were reassuring. Hank threw on some more coal and they settled in for the long trip. Engine No. 219 was purring like a kitten.

Hank broke the silence. "Hey, Charlie, at the risk of sounding like a fool, there's something I want to ask you."

"It's too late for that, but go ahead," Charlie chuckled.

"You've got a point there. Seriously, have you ever heard any stories about ghost riders on trains?"

"Why do you ask?" Charlie responded.

Taking a deep breath, Hank reluctantly pushed on: "Well, you ain't gonna believe this. When I hopped the first train out of Thurmond, there were two hobos already aboard. One was a friendly old, black man, who called himself Boxcar Billy. He introduced his side-kick as Night Rider. I remember Billy laughing and asking me if I played that guitar or was it just for looks. The three of us ended up playing music until late into the night. Billy was playing an old harmonica, and Night Rider kept the rhythm with a pair of beat-up drumsticks. We passed my flask around 'til it was empty and had a good-old time. Finally, all three of us settled into the hay and tried to get some shut-eye. I slept fitfully but definitely knew the train did not stop anytime during the night. The early morning light woke me from a stupor. Needless to say, I was feeling a little rough. I glanced around the boxcar, but there was no sign of Billy or Night Rider. They were just gone. That freaked me out. I tried to shake it off, but the memory of that night keeps haunting me."

"Man, that's really bizarre. I remember my dad telling stories about two old hobos called Boxcar Billy and Night Rider, who used to ride the trains up and down the lines. The weird thing is they've been dead for over twenty-five years now. This is the story I heard: It was a dark night, and the two, old friends miscalculated and jumped off a moving train at the wrong place. The steep embankment where they jumped was nothing but large boulders. A hunter found their mangled bodies at the bottom of a deep ravine covered with Kudzu vines. Supposedly, the only thing they found on Billy was a beat-up old harmonica in his overall's pocket." Charlie continued, "I've heard the night watchmen tell stories about hearing a bluesy harmonica sound coming from some of the parked boxcars. When they checked it out, no one was there."

Hank let out a big sigh. "I'd never believed in ghosts or spirits, but I certainly do now. Do you think they exist in some kind of dimension outside of our normal space and time? I certainly don't understand. It's all a big mystery to me. Guess I should just say my thanks to them for getting me through what would have otherwise been a long and difficult night."

"Hank, I don't know nothing about spirits and other dimensions, but you can't deny that's some really spooky shit. Best not say anything, because if the boys in the yard get a whiff of this, they'll never stop kidding you."

Twilight was fading and night was falling dark on the landscape. Blustery winds picked up, and shortly afterwards a torrential rain came down making visibility an issue. Running a train at night was always the toughest time, especially in inclement weather.

Charlie pulled out his thermos of coffee and said, "I'll take the first watch, so try and get some rest. I'll wake you if I need you."

Hank settled down in the uncomfortable bunk, but sleep never came. He was still thinking about the ghost riders. Finally, he got up and decided to have some coffee. Hank checked the gauges and took control of the train. It was almost dawn and the rain had stopped, except for a light drizzle. A layer of fog blanketed the countryside, and Hank almost did not see a ten-point buck run across the tracks. The panicked deer barely made it across in time. Hank was happy that the big stag would live to rut again another day.

As they approached the Shoals Creek Bridge, Hank started throttling the engine down. The original wood trestle and truss bridge was built in the early 1800s at the height of over two-hundred feet. Crossing that bridge made Hank feel a bit apprehensive. He reduced the speed and carefully started the journey across. Charlie was up and observed the crossing.

When they reached the other side, Hank said, "Did that bridge feel like it had a lot of sway?"

Charlie rubbed his sleepy eyes and said, "Man, I was thinking the same exact thing. I'll make sure to write that in our trip report."

Finally, they arrived at the yard in Fayetteville. Hank decided he would drop in and see how Nessa and Eileen were getting along. Besides, he needed food and sleep.

He invited Charlie but he declined. "Thanks for the invite, but I've got business to take care of. I'll see you in the morning for breakfast before we commence our long trek back to Nashville. This trip will be much slower, though. We'll be hauling one-hundred hopper cars loaded with tons of black diamonds [Term used to describe hematite coal]."

CHAPTER 18

Fairy Tale

$\mathcal{L}$ ouise had left her draperies open to allow the light of sunrise to stream through her window. A luminous, golden radiance filled her room with hope and the promise of a new day. She replayed her debut performance in her mind critiquing every song. Then without warning, her attention turned to Sonny. Thinking about him and last night gave her the jitters. Louise thought, *Sonny's charming and flamboyant style is certainly appealing, but on the other hand, perhaps I'm just feeling lonely and vulnerable.*

Louise stepped out of the tub and wrapped a luxurious towel around her wet body. She dressed casually, adding a cloak of optimism, and went downstairs where Sonny's driver was waiting.

Upon arrival she knocked lightly on Sonny's office door. He enthusiastically opened it with a big smile. "Good morning, Louise! Welcome to my office. I appreciate the fact that you are punctual. May I get you a cup of coffee and a croissant?"

"Yes. Thanks. Coffee sounds great."

Sonny led her into the conference room, "Let's get started, shall we?" He proceeded to inform her how Sound Production Studio could help achieve her career goals. He took a sip of coffee and handed her a contract. "Please take your time going over the contract. If you have any questions or requests, please just let me know. Afterwards, if you agree and sign, I would like to record a sample of your music to send to my friend Mike Fritzel, the owner of Chez Paree in Chicago. He's always looking for new talent. Also,

I intend to send a copy to The Cotton Club in New York. You will need to develop a following in order to generate press, but that's part of my job."

Sonny was apparently buzzed from the coffee. "Be thinking about what song you would like to record—one that best represents you. I'll give you some time to look over the contract; and whenever you're ready, I'll be in my office directly across the hall." Without even giving Louise the time to speak, he stepped into the hallway and closed the door.

Louise admired all the personally autographed photos hanging on the wall, including Lead Belly and Robert Johnson, Billie Holiday and Louis Armstrong. Louise tried to imagine her photo among them. She chuckled to herself. *I'm having delusions of grandeur.*

Picking up the musician's contract, she began to read it slowly. All those legal words seemed so lengthy and unnecessary to portray such a simple thing. She took a deep breath and read over the scope of the contract as well as the duties and rights of agents. She underlined the areas where she had questions and then opened the door and motioned for Sonny to enter.

Her palms were moist, and she spoke with a false yet convincing bravado. "Sonny, before I consider signing the contract, I have a couple of concerns: First, I'll only sign for one year and not three. Let's give ourselves this option in case things don't work out for either of us; Second, you have listed that your compensation would be twenty-five percent of the gross revenue. Cody mentioned that the agent's fee should be no less than ten percent and no more than twenty. If we're going to enter this partnership, then I suggest we meet in the middle at fifteen percent. Also, I've signed a contract with the hotel that I must honor. I'll leave that to you and Cody to work out. If you agree to these terms, then I'll be honored to sign."

Sonny leaned confidently back in his chair. He smiled and said, "Louise, you are not only beautiful but you're smart as well. I'll agree to the decrease in percentage, however, our contracts are usually for three years. That's because we invest a lot time and money in marketing our musicians. Would you consider two years instead?"

With that, Louise responded, "Yes, I think that's a good compromise."

"Looks like we've reached an agreement." After signing the contract, Sonny presented her with the Montblanc pen, "Please accept this pen as a token of our partnership. Hopefully it will inspire you to write even more creative lyrics for your songs." As they were walking down the hall, he continued, "Don't worry about Cody. He's a good friend and we'll find a way to honor your contract."

"Thanks. This is a really nice pen, and a great memento commemorating the significance of our partnership. I will definitely put it to good use."

"Louise, as our newest protégé, welcome to your new home, Sound Production Studio." Sonny pulled an envelope from his jacket pocket. "As noted on the contract, here's an advance to help take care of your expenses and wardrobe. I look forward to working with you for what is hopefully a long career. Now, let's record your demo tapes."

Louise tuned her instrument as Sonny adjusted the mic to accommodate her voice. "I'm really excited to see how your sound comes across on tape. I believe your voice will move easily in terms of pitch. You possess a hypnotic quality that captures and holds the attention of your audience. Just relax and be yourself, and let that charming voice of yours fly free."

Louise recorded a selection of songs so that Sonny would have a variety to choose from. After finishing her final one, they listened to the playback and her voice came through strong and regal. He was very happy and pleased with the results.

The minute Louise left Sonny's office, he picked up the phone and called his friend Mike on his private line at the Chez Paree. Mike answered the phone and heard Sonny's enthusiastic voice. "Hey, Mike, what about having lunch with me tomorrow? I just signed a new talent, Louise O'Neill, and she's going to blow you away. I was thinking about flying up in the morning and delivering her demo tapes in person."

"Sure, that sounds good. I'm looking forward to seeing you. This Louise must be something if you're personally bringing the tapes."

"Just you wait. Thanks, Mike. I'll see you tomorrow."

Sonny possessed a passion for flying. He owned a 1933 Northrop Delta eight-passenger plane that he kept in a hangar at Berry Field Airport. An amendment to the Air Commerce Act disqualified single-engine planes for passenger travel at night and over rough terrain. Due to this Act he was able to purchase the plane for a good price. His Northrop Delta was powered by a Wright SE-1820-F2 nine-cylinder-air-cooled radial piston engine. Delivering 735 horsepower with a speed of 221 mph at a range of 1,650 miles, Sonny could make it to Chicago in a little over two hours. Fortunately, the weather for the next day looked perfect for flying.

"Oh my God, Louise! I can't believe last night. You were amazing. It looks like Sonny has got his eyes on you, girl. Now, Calvin and Sonny are both in love with you. Could you at least give me one of them?" Sadie announced after Louise walked into the boutique.

"You can have them both, I just want my Hank back. I signed a contract this morning with Sonny. He wants to book me in Chicago and New York. I can hardly believe it."

Sadie responded, "Oh! Louise that's great. You deserve this break. I'm so excited for you. Listen to this: I didn't realize that Carmen was also at The Birdcage last night. She really enjoyed your show and has offered to sponsor you by providing your wardrobe. In exchange you would allow her to advertise that you shop at her boutique exclusively. This could be a big help for you and great publicity for her. What do you think?"

"Wow! This is all coming together like a fairy tale. I would definitely be interested. Ask Carmen if she would like to meet us at The Birdcage tomorrow afternoon for a cocktail."

With enthusiasm Sadie answered, "Hell yes! Let's celebrate."

CHAPTER 19

Lonesome Blues

*H*ank and Charlie arrived in Nashville much later than expected.
Their arduous journey was plagued with breakdowns and delays.

On a straightaway stretch, Hank noticed something lying across the
tracks ahead and powered down the engine. Charlie hopped off the train
and had mercy on a suffering eight-point buck. Apparently, a hunter had
failed to administer a fatal shot. They field-dressed the deer and threw the
carcass into the caboose.

"Tallulah will be thrilled to get this venison," Charlie commented. "She
makes the best roast with potatoes and carrots. Makes me hungry just
thinking about it." They finally arrived at Union Station and submitted
their trip report. Hank got down to business and butchered the deer.
Charlie packaged and labeled each piece. They gave a couple of steaks to
Mr. Johnson, but the remainder would go into their freezer.

After arriving back home, Charlie surprised Tallulah with the fresh
venison. "Sis, you sure are a welcome sight to these tired old railroad
cowboys."

She laughed. "Welcome home, cowboys. I thought y'all were supposed
to be working instead of hunting. Go wash up and come eat. I want to hear
all the stories."

After supper, Tallulah poured some whiskey and raised her glass.
"Cheers! I'm glad y'all are home. There's nothing like sipping a good drink
with friends and family while sitting around a fire. Now, please entertain
me." The cowboys chuckled.

"Hank definitely has the best story, but I'm not sure he wants to share."

Tallulah saw him hesitate and said, "Come on, Hank. Tell me your story."

Hank took a sip of whiskey and obliged. He told her about Boxcar Billy and Night Rider. As he was recollecting the events in his mind, it sounded like he was spinning a tall tale. He knew that he wasn't. He remembered them vividly, like they were real.

"Hank, that is so strange. It gives me goose bumps. Do you believe in ghosts?" Tallulah asked, as she was mesmerized with the story.

He responded, "That's a discussion for another night, 'cause this old boy's gonna hit the sack. Goodnight and thanks for supper. See y'all in the morning." As he stood to leave, Queenie was right beside him.

Tallulah asked, "Would you like for Queenie to stay with you tonight?"

"Well, that's up to her, isn't it?" Queenie barked and ran for the door.

"Guess she answered that question. Goodnight all!"

Hank was tired but he could not sleep. He kept playing scenarios of Louise over and over in his mind like a broken record. He felt that unresolved issues were holding him hostage from moving on with his life. Hank was still very much in love with Louise and wanted her back more than anything. He thought, *I've got to be realistic about my chances of winning her back. If things don't work out, at least she got me out of the mines.*

Then unwillingly, his mind drifted back to his night with Tallulah. *What is it about those eyes of hers? It's like she can see right into my soul. If she were here right now, I would not be able to resist her.* These conflicting feelings created such discord and noise within his head.

Queenie whined and wanted to jump in bed with him. He was not sure how Tallulah would feel about that, but at the moment he didn't care. He was happy to have her company. Queenie settled in, and Hank started petting her; that was all the comfort he needed to finally give up the fight and fall into a deep sleep.

Hank rose with the morning sun feeling rejuvenated and enthusiastic. The idea struck him to leave a note for Louise at The Noel Hotel. He was ruminating about what to say and finally wrote this:

Louise Darling,

Since the day you left, I have been thinking of a way to get you back into my life. Now that I've found you, I can hardly wait to see you again. We have so many things to talk about. How soon can I see you? I'm still madly in love with you.

Hank

Then realizing that he had not left any contact information in the note, Hank thought: *I better think about this. That could mean trouble. What if Tallulah answers the phone when Louise calls? How could I explain that? The hell with it! I'll just go to the hotel and ask to see her.*

Even though it was a chilly and blustery morning, he decided to take Queenie for a long run to the hotel. While jogging, Hank noticed that during his absence most of the trees had lost their leaves. Winter was creeping in. Hank was happy to be out of New River Gorge where the winters were long and brutal. The worst part of living there was the community's isolation from the outside world.

When Hank arrived at The Noel Hotel, he tied Queenie to a rail outside. He walked up to a persnickety-looking man at the front desk whose name tag read "Mr. Biden." He was balding with strands of hair swept over to the side and large glasses that were halfway down his nose.

Hank asked politely, "Sir, would you please ring Louise O'Neill's room?"

Mr. Biden gave Hank a condescending look. "You had best move along before I call the police. We don't cater to your kind."

Hank started to get angry but stuffed it inside. "Sir, it's important that I contact her. May I please at least leave her a note?"

Mr. Persnickety turned his back and walked away without an acknowledgement. *What a jerk!* Hank left the hotel not knowing that Louise was enjoying her morning breakfast just mere feet from him.

Hank burned off his frustrations by running back to the house. Queenie loved it and stayed in step on his right flank. Charlie was sitting in the kitchen reading the morning newspaper, and Tallulah was cooking breakfast when they walked through the back door—both out of breath.

"Hey, man, what's the long face about this morning?" Charlie asked.

Hank shared what happened at the hotel. "That little bastard. Who does he think he is? Don't worry, Hank. We'll find a way to get to her."

Tallulah interjected, "Hank, let me try a more subtle approach. Perhaps, as a woman, that jerk will be more forthcoming with information."

Charlie chuckled, "Trust me. Tallulah could get the Pope to reveal all his secrets." They all laughed, and Hank felt more optimistic.

"Thanks, Tallulah, I would definitely appreciate that."

"Sure, anything for my cowboys. Since you both have today off, why don't I pack a picnic lunch and let's drive over to Radnor Lake? We could hike the Garnier Ridge Trail. There's abundant wildlife in that area this time of year."

"Sis, that's a great idea."

Queenie started barking, and Tallulah reached down to pet her. "Yes. You can come too."

Hank thought, *A long hike in nature sounds like the perfect antidote for these lonesome blues of mine.*

CHAPTER 20

Reckless Abandon

Louise was on her way to meet Sadie and Carmen in the lounge when she decided to stop by Cody's office. After knocking gently on his door, she heard him say, "Please come in."

"Hello, Cody. I just wanted to make you aware that I've signed a contract with Sonny."

"Louise, when I heard you sing, I knew that you were going to be a success. I've spoken with Sonny, and we've found a way that you can honor both your contracts. I'm sure he'll explain it to you in greater detail. So, don't worry; everything's fine."

"Cody, thanks for being so understanding and taking a chance with me."

"It is my pleasure. Oh! I heard from Calvin yesterday, and he's coming for your next performance."

Louise's face lit up. "That's great. I look forward to seeing him again. Goodbye, Cody. We'll talk soon."

Then she left to meet Sadie and Carmen in the lounge where she took an adjoining bar stool. Sadie graciously made the introductions. Carmen extended her hand. "Louise, I saw your performance and you were fantastic. It's such a pleasure to meet you." As they ordered cocktails she continued, "Sadie said she explained my idea about providing your gowns, and you have agreed."

"Thanks, Carmen. I love your idea; I'd be honored to accept the arrangement. The fringe benefit is, I've made a new friend." Louise immediately liked Carmen upon seeing her beautiful smile and hearing her contagious laugh.

"Thanks, Louise. Let's have dinner. Tonight, it's my treat."

The ladies moved to a window table overlooking a lush courtyard. Once they were seated, the concierge delivered a note to Louise. She opened the card and read aloud:

Louise, may I have the pleasure of dining with you tomorrow evening? Please meet me in penthouse number 1213 at 7:00 p.m. I have exciting news to share with you. Fondly, Sonny.

Carmen said, "I think this calls for a bottle of champagne."

"Yes, champagne for our real friends and real pain to our sham friends," Louise said, igniting laughter around the table.

Louise awoke to a chilly and rainy day. She pulled the covers over her head to ward off the heartsick feeling that filled her with dread. Dewdrops of rain trickled down the windowpanes as if they too were weeping. The luxury that surrounded her only seemed to enhance her sadness. *Hank, I would trade it all to be back in your arms again.* A pang of regret for having left him alone consumed her. She could imagine his trudging to the mine in the snow with his head hung low, and then coming home to a cold, dark, and empty house. That thought crushed her as she wallowed in guilt. *How could I have been so selfish after everything he's done for me?* Salty tears came again uninvited, and she rolled into a fetal position and surrendered to them.

In the midst of her depression, there were rare moments of resistance gleaming out from her melancholy. With fortitude, Louise climbed out of bed and splashed cold water on her puffy eyes. She spent the day in her room resting and finished writing "Tracks From Nowhere." The upbeat music from a local radio station helped to lift her spirits.

Near the approach of evening, the rain stopped and sunshine filtered through the sheer drapes. Dust motes danced in the waves of the fading light. Louise smiled, *The sunshine seems to have replaced the storm that has been raging in my heart. I'm done with feeling regret. Regret is keeping me a prisoner of negative thoughts and emotions. From now on I'm going to focus on gratitude and the exciting news that Sonny has to share.*

Louise dressed and applied makeup lightly from the samples that Sadie had given her. Gazing into the mirror, she felt self-confidant and was looking forward to dinner with Sonny.

Arriving fashionably late, Louise approached door number 1213 and knocked lightly. She fidgeted nervously with her hair until Sonny answered the door looking irresistibly handsome.

"Good evening, Louise. It's so good to see you."

"It's good to see you too, Sonny. Thanks for the invitation."

He escorted Louise through the tastefully appointed apartment to a roof-top terrace. A table for two was elegantly set in front of a roaring fireplace. Candles and roses adorned the table along with crystal stemware and white porcelain china. Sonny seated Louise by the warmth of the fire. She marveled at the dazzling panoramic view overlooking downtown and the river. Sonny popped the cork on a bottle of Veuve Clicquot champagne and poured two flutes. "The French think it's rude and crass that Americans like to pop corks. I, on the other hand, happen to think it's a lot of fun. Cheers, Louise!"

She laughed. "Who cares what the French think? Cheers!" His easy manner helped her feel more relaxed.

An artfully arranged charcuterie board sat on the table between them. Sonny spread Brie Cheese upon a cracker. Hesitating for a few moments, as though not to reveal too much too soon, he spoke professionally: "Louise, I flew your demo tapes to Chicago yesterday and personally met with Mike Fritzel. He was very impressed as I felt he would be. Mike wants to book you at the Chez Paree in two weeks."

Then, almost apologetically, Sonny added, "I know this is short notice. Don't worry, though, we'll have you ready. What do you think? It's pretty exciting, huh?"

Louise took a sip of the cold champagne and felt the warmth from the fire. "Sonny, I'm speechless. It's hard for me to believe the wonderful opportunities that have come my way. My heart is filled with gratitude." A tear of joy escaped and silently rolled down her cheek. Sonny reached across the table and took her hand. "Louise, you deserve this. I knew the moment I heard you sing that this is your destiny."

She brushed the tear aside. "I'm thrilled to have this chance, and I promise I'll do my best to live up to your expectations."

With the first bottle of Veuve empty, Sonny said, "Let's piss the French off again, shall we?" Another cork went sailing off the rooftop into the night, and they both laughed. As the champagne flowed, so did the conversation. Louise was interested in learning more about Sonny.

Her curiosity was piquing so she asked. "Sonny, you mentioned that you flew to Chicago, do you own an airplane?"

"Yes, I do. Flying is my greatest passion. I'll take you up sometime if you like."

She nodded with excitement and asked another question. "I saw your jacket and helmet hanging in the foyer. Do you also own a motorcycle?"

"Yes, I have a 1936 Harley-Davison EL Knucklehead. There's nothing quite like cruising the country roads on a motorcycle. Forgive me, Louise, for talking so much. Let's eat."

Sonny raised the silver dome covering the plates of filet mignons topped with lump crabmeat and Béarnaise sauce with sides of roasted potatoes and grilled asparagus. Louise smelled the aroma. "Oh! My! That food looks delicious."

The fire crackled and sent sparks flying out the chimney creating a romantic ambiance. After dinner, Louise excused herself to freshen up. She was feeling rather bubbly but very relaxed. Her worries seemed to have flown off the rooftop with the corks. When she returned to the table, there was a bluesy jazz song, featuring a saxophone, playing on WSM radio.

Sonny stood and bowed slightly. "May I have this dance?"

Throwing caution to the wind, Louise smiled and took his extended hand. They started moving in unison to the hypnotic beat. Having Sonny's arms around her felt reassuring. Her cares and inhibitions seemed to melt away along with her resistance. They danced close without saying a word— letting their bodies do all the talking. His hands gently caressed her defined and lightly muscled back. He pulled her close and removed the decorative comb from her hair allowing her copper locks to fall free.

He breathed in the scent of her and felt an unabated yearning. *This woman thrills me and terrifies me at the same time.* He gently raised her chin and looked into her eyes, thinking, *I could swim in those beautiful eyes.* As they danced, he kissed her neck and found his way to her luscious mouth.

Louise abruptly pulled back. "I'm sorry, Sonny. I can't do this. Could you please just hold me for a while?"

Lovingly, he wrapped his arms around her. "Louise, it's all right. Forgive me for being so forward. I would never do anything intentionally that would make you feel uncomfortable." They danced for the longest time entwined in each other's arms just swaying to the music.

The longing inside Louise could not be denied. *Damn it, I'm so tired of hurting and feeling lonely. Here goes reckless abandon.* She looked into his eyes and then kissed him passionately. Sonny felt a shudder spasm throughout his body. He picked her up and carried her into the bedroom as she let herself completely surrender. He unzipped her long dress and let it fall to the floor. Sonny delicately loosened the straps to her silk slip, and it fell to the floor as well. He laid her on the bed, and the reins of consciousness slipped away from both of them. He caressed and kissed her all over—drinking in her essence. Their passion kept pulsing while building up to a crescendo until they both released and pure ecstasy washed over their bodies.

They lay in each other's arms, relishing in their spent passion. Louise kissed him on the cheek and said, "Sonny, you need to know my situation. You are the only man besides my husband that I've ever lain with. Yes, I'm married, but I left him to come to Nashville." It was not easy for Louise but she continued, "I still have feelings for him, but I'm just not sure how our situation is going to turn out. My life as a coal miner's wife was very different than it is now. We had little and struggled just to survive. I had to hock my grandmother's diamond ring to get the money for a train ticket here." Louise sighed. "So you see, all this beauty and luxury is quite sudden and foreign to me. It's a lot for a girl to wrap her head around. Tomorrow I'm planning to take the train back to Thurmond to retrieve my ring. I'm going to see my husband while there to hopefully resolve our situation one way or another. It's a long story but I hope you understand."

"Sweet, Louise, I've only known you for a short time, but I care for you more than I have a right to. This is not the pillow talk I was hoping for, but I do understand. Just please come back. That's all I ask."

Louise kissed him tenderly on the cheek. "Don't worry. I promise I'll be back and ready for Chicago. Sonny, just know that I don't feel any remorse about tonight."

The next morning, Louise purchased a roundtrip ticket to Thurmond. She boarded the train and made her way to the proper assigned seat. After placing her bag in the overhead bin, she made herself comfortable. A new song was rolling around in her head. She pulled out her pen and paper to try and capture it. As Louise started writing, the chain of thoughts from her original idea now seemed sporadic and unconnected. She kept rearranging the phrasing to give it more meaning, rhyme, and continuity. Deep in thought, she was vaguely aware of the conductor walking down the aisle collecting tickets. Louise stared out the window in serious concentration as the panoramic scenery rolled by. Nonchalantly, she held her ticket up to the conductor. He took it from her extended hand and moved down the aisle. Louise thought, *If only I could find that one word that rhymes and ties the song together emotionally.*

CHAPTER 21

Secret to Confess

$\mathcal{H}$ank and Charlie arrived at the depot early Monday morning. A frost lay over the frozen ground like fine snow. They stomped the accumulation off their boots and walked into the station. With sleepy eyes and coffee in hand, they examined the assignment board. Charlie was headed to Chattanooga, but Hank's name was not on the board. Mr. Johnson approached them, glad that Hank had arrived. "Hank, I need a big favor. My conductor on the passenger train to Thurmond has a medical emergency and can't work today. I need you to fill-in for him."

"Sure thing, Sir. Anything to help out."

Mr. Johnson responded, "I appreciate the team work." He handed Hank a training manual for conductors. "Here, study this list of duties as a conductor. You'll be fine, and the experience will be good for your resume. There's a uniform for you in the locker room."

Hank read over the information: Make sure the train is in compliance with all orders, signals, rules, and regulations. Stamp tickets, maintain a safe and orderly environment, assist passengers when necessary, and alert them of upcoming scheduled stops. He thought, *I can do this. It'll be a nice change of pace.* With confidence, he boarded the train for a final inspection. When everything was in order, he stepped onto the platform and loudly announced, "All aboard!

Hank was casually walking down the aisle chatting with the passengers while collecting their tickets. He glanced to the next seat and right before his eyes sat Louise. He was stunned, and it took a moment to recapture his composure. Hank wanted to say something to her, but she seemed distracted, gazing out the window. As he took her ticket, his heart was beating wildly, like a drum, and the palms of his hands became sweaty. He felt dizzy and disoriented. Hank could not imagine what Louise was doing on the train headed to Thurmond. His crazed mind tried to figure out how best to deal with this surprising development. Hank thought, *I can't believe my lucky stars to be the conductor on this train. What were the chances of this happening?*

After collecting all the passengers' tickets, he went directly to see Jesse, the porter. Hank explained his situation and asked if there were any vacant sleeper cabins available.

"Sho nuf, man. Anything fo you, Mr. Hank. Cabin number 13 is empty."

"Thanks, Jesse, I owe you one. I need you to deliver a note to my wife. Please escort her and any luggage she has back to the cabin."

Jesse smiled, and the light reflected off his gold tooth. "I'd be happy to, Mr. Hank."

Hank sat down to compose a note. After writing Louise's seat number on the folded paper, he gave it to Jesse for delivery.

"Excuse me, ma'am, but I has a message fo you," Jesse said to Louise as politely as possible.

She was very surprised and thought, *Who could possibly be sending me a note?* Regardless, she accepted the note and opened it. A look of shock registered on her face as she read: *My Dearest Louise, Please allow Jesse, the porter, to escort you to cabin number 13 where I'll be waiting. Your Loving Husband, Hank.*

Louise sat still for a moment feeling overwhelmed, and her breathing became heavy. She looked up nervously at Jesse. He smiled and invited her to come with him as he grabbed her bag. Speechless, she stood and followed him nonetheless. Once they were at the door, Jesse took his leave. While standing there she thought, *How is this possible? What is Hank doing on this train headed to Thurmond?*

Louise took a deep breath and knocked on the cabin door. Hank answered, looking very handsome in his conductor uniform, and stepped aside to let her enter. He stood in a rigid, almost militaristic pose as if afraid to breathe.

There they were, face to face, feeling shock and awkwardness in the small space. They hugged in an unfamiliar and cumbersome way.

"Hank, what are you doing here? Do you work for the railroad now? I must say that this is a big shock and surprise to see you on this train wearing a uniform. I'm happy to see that you've left the mines," Louise babbled nervously.

Hank invited her to sit down and replied, "Yes, but I normally work as an engineer on freight trains. I'm wondering what you're doing headed back to Thurmond in your fancy clothes. I thought you made your escape never to return." Hank was so excited to see her, but his sarcastic tone surprised even him.

"I'm actually on my way to retrieve my grandmother's ring out of hock. I was also planning on seeing you, but here you are. Hank, we need to talk and reach a resolution. It's not fair for either of us to continue this way with our marriage in limbo."

Hanks words rushed out, "I couldn't agree with you more. Louise, I was there at your debut. I wanted to come say hello afterwards, but you were surrounded by men. There was one man who was paying special attention to you. Who was that man kissing on you?" Hank's jealousy was kicking in, and the volume of his voice was rising along with his Irish temper.

Louise had never responded well when being talked to in that manner, so she sarcastically replied: "Hank O'Neill, I begged you to come with me and you refused. Do you think I wanted to leave without you? No, I didn't, but you left me with no other option." Louise's voice was also rising above the clickety-clack of the rails as she continued her tirade, "You made your choice, and I've made mine. Don't you dare come down on me now. You have no right to be angry with me."

"Well, please forgive me, your highness," Hank caustically replied. He turned to leave and offered, "Please feel free to remain in this cabin for the duration of your trip, compliments of the railroad." He slammed the door and stormed off fuming. He found a private place in the caboose and tried to calm himself from his unresolved raw emotions. *I was so excited to see Louise face to face, but I acted like a complete jealous jerk. I've definitely got to be more prepared for round two, and there's only one place to start, with a heart-felt apology.*

Louise sat in the lonely cabin with tears streaming down her cheeks. *Damn it, Hank O'Neill! We didn't handle that very well, did we? Man, you drive me crazy, so why do I still want you? If you had just come with me, we could have avoided all this pain.*

Anger flashed through her mind at the thought of Nessa. *Nessa is the reason Hank wouldn't leave. That miserable and spiteful old woman doesn't deserve a loyal and caring son like Hank.* Then she wondered how Hank had escaped his mother and New River Gorge. So many unanswered questions swirling through her brain. Louise sat in silence thinking about how to handle their predicament. The miles rocked on, leaving her with no more wisdom or insight than before. She pulled down the shade, grabbed a pillow, and decided to wait for Hank's return. This discussion was far from over.

☙❧

Jesse was in the dining car when Hank found him. He kindly asked, "Jesse, would you mind bringing two dinners and a bottle of white wine to cabin number 13 around seven o'clock?"

"Sho nuf, Mr. Hank. I gotcha covered."

Hank proceeded to the cabin and knocked lightly on the door.

Louise composed herself and responded curtly, "Come in!"

Hank entered and knelt down to her seated position. He gently took her hand and looked at her with remorseful eyes. "Louise, please forgive me. I let my emotions and jealousy get the better of me. Please, darling, can we try and talk again? Woman, you have no idea how much I've missed you."

Louise's eyes watered and she answered, "Hank, please sit beside me. Let's have a drink, because sometimes the truth needs a laxative." She reached for her flask and offered it to him.

"I really shouldn't because I'm on duty, but since this is an extenuating circumstance, why not?"

They took a drink for courage. As the fire traveled downward, they seemed to relax into each other's company. Hank looked lovingly at Louise. "When you sang 'Grace' the other night, I was overcome with emotion. You know that song gets me every time. Honestly, I've never been prouder of you."

"I'm so glad you were there at my debut. I wish I had known. You have no idea how nervous I was. When I left the stage, I blew a kiss for you."

Hank smiled gratefully at her. She continued, "Hank, that man you asked about is Sonny Reinheart, my producer and agent. He's booked me in Chicago at The Chez Paree in less than two weeks. This is my big break."

Hank reached over and raised the shade to let the evening light in.

"Louise, I'm so happy for you. I've always known that you have a great talent. Congratulations, darling! You deserve this. I sincerely hope you make it big. I'll never forgive myself for not coming with you. All I can do now is ask for your forgiveness." Hank paused for a few moments, and the pain of their separation showed on his face. "Louise, I've been so lost without you. You must know that I'm still madly in love with you. I'll do anything to get you back and keep you in my life. I just need to know if there's a chance we can ever be together again. Please respect our marriage enough to tell me the truth."

Louise was touched deeply by Hank's sincerity. Powerful emotions stirred within her. "Hank, you and I have always been honest with each other; so yes, I'll be honest with you now. Sonny and I have been seeing each other, and we were intimate once. I was very lonely and feeling vulnerable. I know that's no excuse, but I'm not offering one. It happened. I can't change that. I did tell Sonny that I still have feelings for you and that I intended to see you on this trip."

Silence prevailed in the cabin. All they could hear were the sounds the train made as the sun was setting across the landscape. Louise took her hands and turned his face towards her. "Hank, I have missed you terribly. Leaving you was the hardest thing I've ever done in my life."

Hank grabbed the flask and took another swig. "Louise, are you in love with him? I need to know where I stand."

She returned his steel gaze. "No, but I have been infatuated with him. Sonny is a good man. He's very charming; and frankly I have enjoyed his attention, but I am not in love with him." Hank released a big sigh and Louise continued, "I can't promise you anything right now. All I know is I have to follow my dream and see where it goes. I don't have the right to ask you to wait and see. That wouldn't be fair. You have to know that I still love you very much, but a lot of things have changed since we were last together."

Hank was still reeling from her confession. He felt as though he had been kicked in the gut. The image of another man's hands on her body made him crazy. He thought, *I certainly have no right to feel betrayed or be angry with Louise. I have my own secret to confess.*

Right on time there was a light knock on the cabin door. Hank slid the door open, and Jesse delivered their dinners along with a chilled bottle of Chardonnay. Hank shook Jesse's hand and slipped him a bill. He smiled big in return. "Hope you folks enjoy yo dinner."

Hank smiled mischievously and poured Louise a glass of wine. "To continue this conversation, we're gonna need more laxative."

As the train rolled on into the night, they ate in silence. Hank was pondering how he was going to come forth with his own confession. After they finished eating, Louise poured another glass of wine and said, "Here's to the truth. May it set us free."

Hank couldn't decide if Louise was regarding him with suspicious eyes or if it was his own guilt he was feeling. Regardless, he felt extremely nervous. After taking a deep breath, his words came flying out. "Darling, I was devastated the day I came home from work to an empty house and found your letter. Without food or sleep, I somehow dragged my arse through the miserable days that followed. One particular morning I arrived at the mine and just knew that I could no longer work there; but more importantly, I knew in my heart that I had to find you at all cost. So, you were my motive for leaving the mines. I understand now how much you desired to have a better life for the both of us."

As night descended, Hank adjusted the lighting in the cabin. "I went straight to see Mother and told her I was leaving to find you. You can imagine her response. To my surprise, Aunt Eileen was there. The good news is that Nessa is going to move in with Eileen. I had already made my decision to leave, but that bit of news made it all the sweeter."

Louise reached over and embraced Hank. She said apologetically, "Hank, I'm so sorry. Please forgive me. I know that I hurt you really bad. I was so scared and hurting badly myself, but I knew that I had to go or I was going to lose my mind in that awful place."

Hank settled back in his seat. "I know, darling. The truth is, I never blamed you for leaving. I blamed myself for not going with you."

The steam whistle blew and the train began slowing down. Hank instinctively knew they were making the approach for the Shoal Creek Bridge. As the train started the crossing, Hank said, "This bridge makes me nervous every time we cross it." Then he told Louise his story of how he left New River Gorge and made his way to Nashville. Finally, there was nothing left to tell except for the hardest part—the secret that gnawed at his soul. *Louise was so direct and honest, but how can I tell her about Tallulah?*

Louise noticed his hesitation. "Hank, is there something more you need to tell me?" He turned to face her and ran his fingers through his dark hair. "Yes, my love! You are not the only one who has been infatuated with someone else. After arriving in Nashville, Charlie suggested I move into his sister's carriage house and help her by performing some house repairs 'til I got on my feet."

Hank was at a loss for words as he stumbled for an explanation. "Charlie's sister, Tallulah, is really a great gal. Her husband was killed in a coal-mining accident a couple of years ago, and she moved to Nashville to be near Charlie. She mentioned that she'd not been with anyone since her husband's untimely death. The loneliness got the better of both of us, and one night we slept together. When I awoke in her arms, the guilt overwhelmed me. Afterwards, I was a coward and avoided her." Hank paused for a moment, trying to find an appropriate way to continue. "Louise, Tallulah has helped me a lot and has encouraged me not to give up on winning you back. She has tirelessly helped me search for you. You two could be best friends, if you'd give her a chance. I'm really sorry, darling. Can you ever forgive me?"

Louise grabbed a lace handkerchief out of her handbag to dry the tears that were rolling down her face. It was her time to feel she'd been kicked in the gut. She wanted to be angry but knew she had no right to be. The thought of Hank making love to another woman was unbearable. She reached out, and he embraced her as she sobbed irrepressibly on his shoulder. They just held each other for the longest time accompanied only by the sounds of the train and their shallow breathing.

Hank kissed her and whispered in her ear, "My darling, it's really late. Why don't you try and get some sleep? I'm still on duty, so I have to go back to work. Meet me at 7:00 a.m. in the dining car and we'll have breakfast together."

In her sniffly voice she replied, "Hank, what have we done to each other? It hurt like hell to hear about Tallulah, but thank you for having the courage to speak the truth."

He kissed her on the forehead. "Louise, my darling. I love you so much. Let's talk later. Now please try and get some rest." He wanted to stay with her so badly, but duty called. On his way out the door, he bowed and then blew her a kiss. She laughed out loud at his comic imitation of her. Louise thought, *Hank has always known how to make me laugh.*

Neither of them had slept, but at 7:00 a.m. they were seated across from each other in the dining car. The hot coffee seemed to bring them back to life. Louise took a big sip and said, "Hank, after you left me last night I did a lot of thinking. I have an exciting idea I want to share with you. I absolutely want you to come with me to Chicago. It could be so much fun. We lost each other once, but now we have a second chance to be together.

What do you think?" She recognized that worried look on Hank's face, and it was not the look she was hoping for.

"I have a great job in Nashville and people depend on me. The railroad has been really good to me. I can't just quit and let them down like that." Hank also recognized her look and knew that her temper was rising.

Louise glared at him with angst in her eyes. The pain and rejection from their last time together felt all too familiar. "Damn you, Hank O'Neill. Why is it you're always choosing someone or something else over me? You are loyal to a fault."

Hank put a finger to his mouth to quieten her, but she ignored him and continued. "You said you would do anything to get me back and keep me in your life. Was that just bullshit? Here I am sitting right in front of you, and all you seem to care about is your honor and obligations and not letting other people down. What about me, Hank? I thought you loved me. When am I ever going to be your first choice?"

Reeling from her speech, Hank sat there devastated. Quietly, he was thinking that perhaps Louise was right and he would talk with Mr. Johnson about a leave of absence.

Louise was waiting for an answer and his hesitation irritated her. "Hank, if you have to think about how you're going to answer that question, then never mind. I'm tired of begging. You've broken my heart for the last time. I know you well enough to understand that you have made your decision. Goodbye, Hank. My lawyer will be contacting you soon."

With tears in her eyes, she rose from the table and stormed off in a huff. By that time, everyone in the dining car was privy to their conservation. Hank was too hurt to be embarrassed. He started after her. "Louise. Please wait! Please, understand..." But she was gone—leaving behind nothing but his broken heart.

Hank was busy with work and did not see Louise again before the train arrived in Thurmond. Once there, he checked in at the station and discovered that he was scheduled to return to Nashville immediately on a black diamond run. Feeling empty, he welcomed the respite. *It's just as well. I need some time alone to process what just happened. Frankly, I've had quite enough of the truth for one night. The truth stings like hell.*

CHAPTER 22

Great Idea

$\mathcal{L}$ ouise checked into the hotel directly across from the train station. Compared to The Noel, it was unkept and depressing. After freshening up a bit, she went straightaway to the pawn shop to claim her heirloom. When the attendant could not find her ring, she became almost frantic. Finally the owner was called and he retrieved her heirloom from a safe. She paid off the loan with interest, and then lovingly slipped the ring on her finger. *Interesting,* Louise thought, when noticing that she had unconsciously slipped the ring on her right hand. *I'm taking that as a sign to let Hank go.*

Thurmond seemed like a surreal nightmare to Louise. She certainly did not feel like the same person who had left there not that long ago. While observing the impoverished people of Thurmond, she saw a glimpse of her former self. *I must find a way to help these forgotten people,* she thought.

Louise spent a restless night in the cheap hotel. When she boarded the morning train, a conductor escorted her back to cabin 13. He said, "Your husband arranged this cabin for you. He left on a run back to Nashville last night. Just ring for the porter if you need anything."

She thanked him and was grateful for the solitude. The fire of her anger was gone and had left her with an unusually low spirit. Louise had not seen Hank since leaving the breakfast table and asked herself why that mattered. Perhaps she did not choose the perfect way to handle their breakfast meeting, but the feelings of rejection were all too fresh in her mind. To make matters worse, she could not get the impression of Hank and Tallulah making love out of her head. It was like a bad movie that kept playing over and over. Louise was surprised at how much Hank's confession had affected her. The thought of those two tangled up together haunted her unbearably. Exhausted from having her own private pity party, Louise laid down her weary head and wanted nothing more than for her trip to be over.

꙰

When Louise arrived in Nashville Sonny was there to pick her up at the station. He was all smiles and was being his usual optimistic self; but today, she found that somehow annoying. Sonny put his arm around her and said, "So, how did things go in Thurmond?"

She looked at him with sad eyes. "Sonny, I don't mean to sound rude, but I'm very tired. I've hardly slept in three nights. I just want to take a nap. Can we talk later?"

He removed his arm from her shoulder. "Sure, take your time. I do want to let you know that one of Chez Paree's entertainers has cancelled because of strep throat. The good news is they want you in Chicago a week early. You have just a couple days until your next performance at The Noel, so you're going to be a busy lady. I would like to personally fly you to Chicago, if that's all right with you. Get some rest, Louise, and call me when you feel like talking."

Sonny dropped her off at the hotel and she immediately went to her room. She perused the song lineup that Cody had left along with the rehearsal schedule. With fresh goals to occupy her mind and direct her behavior, she turned out the light and crawled between the covers. Tomorrow was beginning to feel more optimistic.

Louise needed a friend to confide in. She telephoned Sadie and invited her for a cocktail at The Birdcage Lounge. "Girl, tell me what's going on. I see you got your ring back." Thinking Hank was still living in Thurmond, Sadie just had to ask if she had talked to him.

"Sadie, I don't even know if I can talk about it. Order us a drink, would you? Make mine a double. It's so good to see you. Let's just say I got derailed, but I'm back on track again. Pun intended!" They both shared a laugh, and Louise started to be more at ease.

"Hey, I heard your next performance is already sold out. You need to come in tomorrow and pick out a gown." The thought of a full house excited Louise. She smiled and felt the pain recede into the shadows. *Gosh, it sure feels good to be back in Nashville. Nothing is going to stop me now, not even the memory of Hank.*

Rehearsals went extremely well, and Louise felt more assertive. She worked tirelessly, pouring her whole heart and soul into making her next show something spectacular. Louise knew that singing was her destiny, and she was not going to squander the opportunities before her. Having her grandmother's ring back reiterated this conviction and gave her courage and determination.

Sonny took Louise to dinner the night before the performance. She spoke candidly with him. "It's over between me and Hank. It was very painful, and I'm still processing a lot of feelings. I'm not ready to continue our relationship just yet, it wouldn't be fair to you. Right now I just want to focus on my career. I hope you understand."

"Louise, we have time. You're right. Let's just focus on your career. If things work out for us later, then great. If they don't, at least we had one beautiful night together."

Louise leaned in, kissed him on his cheek. "I really do appreciate your understanding." She raised her glass with determination. "Here's to a great trip to Chicago. Let the adventure begin..."

On Saturday night Louise could hear the roaring buzz of conversation and laughter coming from the audience packing The Birdcage Lounge. Cody stepped up to the mic; The crowd grew quieter with anticipation. "Good evening, Ladies and Gentlemen. The last time I had the honor of introducing this talented lady, I mentioned that she was destined for greatness. Soon, she will be performing in Chicago and New York, but tonight she's all ours. Please help me give a heartfelt welcome for the lovely Louise O'Neill."

The audience applauded thunderously as Louise elegantly made her entrance to center stage. She bowed, graciously acknowledging their hearty welcome. She looked stunning in an elegant fit-and-flare silhouette aqua satin gown. The off-the-shoulder fitted bodice was accented with beautiful handmade bead work and sequins that reflected the light.

"The Way You Look Tonight" was Louise's opening number. Her stage fright dissolved as she floated across the stage giving the song her all. Feeling at ease, Louise rolled into the next number, "I've Got You Under My Skin." For her closing song, she had personally selected Robert Johnson's "Sweet Home Chicago." Somehow it just seemed appropriate. It was more challenging for her, but she made the song her own. The emotional response she elicited from the crowd was more than she could have imagined. Before leaving the stage, Louise bowed, and then blew a kiss—a kiss intended for her adoring audience.

After taking a full ten minutes in her dressing room to calm her racing heart and slow the adrenaline pumping through her veins, Louise swept into the grand room straight to Calvin.

He stood to greet her. "My God, darling, you were simply amazing. I already knew that, though, before I ever heard you sing a note." He laughed and patted Sonny on the back. "Has this scoundrel been taking good care of you?"

"Calvin, it's so good to see you again; and yes, Sonny has been a perfect gentleman."

Sonny proposed a toast. "Louise, here's to you, beautiful lady. You were incredible tonight. May the future be prosperous for us all."

Louise took a drink of her champagne and raised her flute. "To Calvin and Sonny, for making this all possible. Salute!"

Glancing towards the next table, Louise asked, "Gentlemen. Would you mind if I invite my friends, Sadie and Carmen, to join us?"

Sonny motioned for the waiter, who escorted the two ladies to their table. When they were comfortably seated and introductions were made, Sonny ordered another bottle of champagne. Corks were not the only thing flying that night. Everyone at the table seemed aware of the romantic sparks between Calvin and Carmen.

As the jovial celebrations swirled around Louise, she felt disconnected from the scene. Sonny reached over and took her hand, and she gave him a sad smile. He knew her heart was breaking, and there was not a thing he could do about it.

Wanting to be alone, Louise excused herself under the pretense of a headache. She was physically drained from her demanding schedule. Also, the daunting reality of leaving Monday morning for Chicago was both exciting and frightening. This should be the happiest time of her life. Instead, she felt tangled up in conflicting emotions. Louise knew that Hank was the root cause. Tears welled in her eyes. She had held back the dam and accomplished so much, but now her resistance was deteriorating.

Sadie went to check on Louise. "Girl, when you left, you sucked all the air right out of the room. Sonny left shortly afterwards. He's so worried about you."

"I know. I've been under a lot of stress lately, and I guess it's finally catching up to me. Performing in Chicago seems a bit overwhelming.

Everything has happened so fast that I haven't even had a chance to catch my breath."

Suddenly, Sadie felt she had the answer. She sat down quickly on the bed next to Louise and grabbed her hand. "I have a great idea. Hopefully you'll think so too. What if I take a few vacation days and go to Chicago with you? Just think of me as your personal attendant."

Louise looked at her in surprise. "You would do that for me?"

"Of course I would, silly. You're my best friend."

The weight of the world lifted as Louise's heart filled with an expression of gratitude for her amazing friend, Sadie.

CHAPTER 23

White Fang

*H*ank pulled back on the throttle as the train approached a section of track that snaked and meandered through twenty miles of dangerous curves. A fast-moving river flowed fiercely on the left side, and a sheer vertical rock cliff flanked the right. As the train rounded a bend, Hank saw what no engineer ever wants to see: a huge rock slide completely covering the tracks.

He yelled, "Emergency! Lock her down!"

Lucas, a new hire, depressed the dead man's handle. Hank used the throttle to bleed the steam, invoking an emergency application. This helped ensure that all available air pressure forced the pistons to apply the brake shoes tight against the train's wheels. There is an inherent problem using this procedure, though. It causes the train to lose power, and it could take hours to rebuild the pressure; but that was the least of their worries.

"Brace for impact!" Hank yelled. The train hissed, wailed, and moaned as it slowly plowed into the rocks and came to a shuddering and screeching halt. They hopped down through the steam and were pleasantly surprised to see that all the wheels had remained on the tracks. That was good news; the bad news was they were stuck in the wilderness without any form of communication.

Quickly taking charge, Hank surveyed their situation. The train was not equipped with the necessary tools for removing a landslide, so their only option was to survive in the wilderness until help arrived. This scenario seemed all too familiar to Hank, as he thought, *At least I don't have to wield an ax.*

Hank instructed Lucas to walk a mile each way and plant a red flag in the middle of the track to signify danger ahead. This was the first trip Hank had partnered with Lucas. He was young and green but was helpful and eager to learn. Hank appreciated his enthusiasm and offered him guidance and encouragement.

After making his way down the steep embankment alongside the tracks, Hank chose a level piece of ground by the stream to set up camp. He cleared a circle and started gathering firewood. Fortunately there were plenty of pine knots from an old felled tree nearby. Without heat from the engine, it was going to be a long, cold night. Once he had gathered firewood, Hank checked their provisions. They had enough food to last a couple of days if rationed carefully, and water was plentiful from the stream.

Daylight was fading fast, so Hank lit the marker lamps on the engine. Thankfully, they had enough kerosene to keep them burning for a while. Upon returning, he opened a couple cans of beans with his Buck Knife and placed them on a rock by the fire, where they quickly heated. Hank and Lucas leaned up against a big log and hungrily ate the warm beans.

The last light of day was gone, and dark descended upon them like a thick blanket. It was a bone-chilling, cold night, and the landscape lay in quiet stillness. A luminous quarter moon gleamed dimly. The twinkling stars added a sense of deceptive harmony to the blue-black sky. Hank gazed up at the heavens and saw a shooting star streaking across the galaxy. Louise used to talk about the universe a lot, but until then Hank had never given it much consideration. He was thinking, *All our petty worries don't mean nothing in the big scheme of things. Humans seem so trivial as compared to the planets and stars, yet here we are. What does it all mean?*

A lone wolf let out a startling howl, and a pack just over the next ridge answered him. A chilling trepidation crept up from the pit of their stomachs, sending shivers down their spines. Hank wished he had some Tennessee sipping whiskey to dispel the cold and uneasiness he felt. He threw another log on the fire. "Lucas, go search the cab and bring back whatever you can find that can be used for shelter and warmth. I'll scavenge for more firewood."

The train sat motionless, yet it was still making settling noises as the cold claimed the mammoth hunk of metal. The fire roared and yellow flames lapped at the sky. They leaned against a big log and chewed on a piece of tough, beef jerky, while Hank asked Lucas how he came to be working on the railroad. Suddenly, the alpha wolf let out another blood-curdling howl, and the pack responded. They were circling much closer.

Hank stood up. "Lucas, don't panic, but the wolves are stalking us. Light a pine-resin knot, because they don't like fire. I'll grab the lantern, and let's carefully make our way back to the engine. Stoke this fire up before we go. We can't afford to let it die down." Hank touched the pistol in his pocket for reassurance. He hoped he would not have to use it on the hungry pack of wolves. He understood that, like himself, they were just trying to survive the night.

Lucas threw a big log on the fire along with some smaller branches. He lit a pine knot, and they started walking towards the engine knowing that running could ensure an immediate attack. Hank looked up on a rock ledge, and there stood the lone alpha wolf in a predatory stance. In the firelight he could vaguely see that the wolf's hackles had risen and his muzzle curled back to expose deadly sharp fangs. They were a few strides from the engine, and the wolves were getting closer.

"Run!" Hank yelled, as they charged up the embankment.

Hank reached the locomotive first, grabbed the handrail, and pulled himself up safely onto the platform. Swiftly, he turned and was in the process of pulling Lucas to safety when the alpha wolf lunged and sank his large canine teeth directly into Lucas's leg. He let out a blood-curdling scream of pain and anguish, but the snarling wolf would not release his prey.

Hank heaved and literally jerked Lucas free from the bone-crushing power of the predator's jaw. Without any forethought, Hank pulled out his pistol and shot the wolf directly between his eyes. He fell with a heavy thud on the rocks below.

The ominous pack was howling incessantly—grieving their fallen leader. Their foreboding howls were maddening as they threw their heads back and pointed their noses towards the dark sky. The pack was in a frenzy and circling the engine. Once the men were safely in the cab, Hank assessed Lucas's injury. When he had jerked him upon the platform, the wolf's powerful fangs ripped open a large, gaping wound. Lucas was visibly shaken and losing blood profusely.

From his first aid training, Hank knew exactly what to do. He grabbed the standard issued American Red Cross First Aid Kit and gave Lucas a Codeine tablet to help with the pain. While cleansing the wound with

Iodine, he noticed that one of the wolf's fangs was embedded deep within the damaged tissue. He removed the canine tooth with a pair of forceps and slipped it into his pocket. Hank cleansed the deep gash and tightly applied a bandage. He instructed Lucas to apply pressure while he looked for something to use as a tourniquet to stop the bleeding. Finding an old rope, he tied it on Lucas's thigh above the wound and used his trusty Buck Knife to tighten the tourniquet. He released the pressure every ten minutes to avoid long-term damage. Hank elevated the injured leg to help slow the flow of blood. His main concern was to keep Lucas stable and from going into shock.

The bleeding had almost stopped, but Lucas was shaking uncontrollably from the frigid cold. Hank stepped outside the cabin and fired a shot into the air. The wolves hastily retreated. He would have to keep a diligent watch during the night because wolves do not give up their prey easily.

Hank patted Lucas on the back. "Don't worry. We're gonna get out of this mess. We've just got to hunker down for a bit 'til help arrives. We need to get back to the fire soon. We'll freeze if we stay here. Remain calm while I get the fire stoked up again, and then I'll come get you."

Lucas with a brave smile replied, "Thanks, man. You're my hero."

After adding more firewood to the fire, Hank realized there probably was not enough to last the night. Then he dragged the dead wolf's body down to the stream and cast it in. He hoped the water would carry the carcass downstream disguising the smell so as not to invite other predators. Once the fire was roaring, Hank carried Lucas to the warmth and got him situated as comfortably as possible. The pain pill was starting to take effect, and Lucas was beginning to relax. The fire was eagerly consuming the wood producing radiant heat, yet they were still cold on their backsides. As they sat silent and shivering beneath a tarp, clouds rolled in covering the sky, and a light snow began to fall. Except for the sounds of the stream, it was so quiet they could actually hear the snowflakes dropping on the dry leaves.

Lucas spoke, shattering the silence. "That was the most scared I've ever been in my whole life. How come you were so cool, Hank?"

"Oh! Trust me, I was plenty scared. Now try to relax and get some sleep, you're gonna need it."

Hank closed his eyes, and his mind drifted to Louise and how stupid he had been to lose her again. He thought, *Instead of spending useless time berating myself, I'm taking Tallulah's advice. Once back in Nashville I'm asking Mr. Johnson for a week off so I can go to Chicago. Then I'm going to surprise Louise with the most beautiful ring I can find. Damn, I love that woman.*

Lucas brought him back to reality when he urgently said, "Hank, can you help me? I need to go to the bathroom."

"There's a giant Hemlock over there, that's about the best we can do," Hank said laughing.

After helping Lucas, Hank took the lantern and went scavenging for more firewood. He was clumsily making his way through the woods when he froze and abruptly stopped in his tracks. He heard the sound of heavy breathing and grunting as something large lumbered through the woods. With nerves on high alert, his heart beat savagely. Hank blew out the lantern hoping to make himself indiscernible then knelt beside a large, sycamore tree. If it were a bear like he thought, he did not want to startle him into an instinctive act of aggression.

Hank sat there shivering. *Bears have a keen sense of smell and most likely the blood from the wolf carcass attracted him. I wonder, though, why ain't that bear in hibernation?* He pulled out the pistol and tried to shake off the feeling of impending danger.

While listening intently, Hank heard the bear heading towards their fire where Lucas was alone and helpless. He circled around and got between the bear and Lucas. There was one bullet left so he had to make it count. From the firelight he saw the bear slap his big paw on the ground and take a predatory stance. The bear was huffing with a deep throaty sound. Hank knew he had to act. Not wanting to kill another beautiful animal, he yelled loudly and shot the pistol into the air. Thankfully, it was enough to make the bear turn and run in the other direction.

Grabbing the lantern and whatever firewood he could carry, Hank made his way back to camp. Lucas looked terrified as Hank dropped the firewood and went to reassure him that they were safe. The snow was coming down harder. Thankfully, they had a tarp for cover. Hank looked at his fob watch. It was four in the morning, and he was very tired. He leaned against the log and thought, *Charlie, I know you're coming for us—but it can't be soon enough.*

Lucas slept fitfully despite taking another Codeine tablet and was having nightmares, as evidenced by his occasional whimpering. Hank rubbed his bloodshot eyes and thought, *Will this night ever end?*

Daylight came slowly as Hank threw the last log on the fire. He was stiff from the cold and his sore muscles ached, but he was happy to have survived the night. Lucas was stirring, and Hank smiled at him: "Good morning. Looks like the snow has stopped. Let me take a look at your injury; the bandage will need changing. Then I'll see what I can scrape up for breakfast. Hey! Lucas! I've got something for you. Here's a fang from the alpha wolf that I removed from your wound. I thought you might want it as a souvenir."

Lucas grinned big. "That's so cool! I'm gonna make a necklace with it, and wear it forever."

Picking up a long stick, Hank placed it first on Lucas's right shoulder and then the left. "I do hereby dub thee *Sir White Fang.*"

Lucas burst out laughing. "I like it! Hey! Hank, you got any more of those pain pills?"

When Charlie learned that Hank's train was late arriving to Nashville, he became concerned and approached Mr. Johnson. "Sir, we need to organize a rescue train. It's not like Hank to be so off schedule. There could have been a landslide or numerous other things could have happened. They could be stranded in this freezing weather. Since there has been no communication, we need to locate them now."

"Charlie, you're my best hire and I trust your judgment. Start organizing a rescue mission immediately. See if old Doc Hannity is available to make the trip. Let me know when you're prepared for departure."

Charlie left the office with a sense of urgency. He immediately started rounding up men and supplies. *Hang on, Hank. We're coming for you.*

CHAPTER 24

That's Ambition

$\mathcal{L}$ouise and Sadie boarded the Northrop Delta on a chilly Monday morning headed to Chicago. Sonny gave a reassuring smile to Louise as she entered the attractively finished cabin. "Ladies," he said. "Make yourselves comfortable. I'll be up front forward of the passenger cabin, but we'll be in constant communication. Buckle up and enjoy the flight."

Sonny settled into the cockpit and put on his headphones. He filed the flight plan and completed the safety check. After inspecting the gauges, he turned on the ignition and pulled out the choke. The robust 735 horsepower Wright Engine powered up and was humming beautifully, yet the passenger cabin was quiet due to the thick panels of soundproofing. As Sonny engaged the throttle, the handsome aircraft moved towards the runway. "Ready for takeoff," he repeated to the tower. They thundered down the runway until the plane's wheels lifted off the ground and they became airborne.

"I'm so glad you're here with me, Sadie. This is quite the adventure. Is this your first time flying? It's definitely mine."

"Yes, it is. I can hardly believe it. Girl, I know you're still in pain over Hank, but just try to enjoy this journey. This is your destiny. Embrace it."

"Sadie, if I'm ever to forget about Hank, then you've got to stop mentioning him. Understand?" Sadie nodded in agreement.

The excitement of takeoff coursed through Louise's veins. Peering out the window with anticipation, she could hardly believe her eyes. Observing earth from the sky gave her a new perspective on life. She felt a sense of peace and calm. As they ascended above the landscape, the panoramic view of the earth became smaller. They rose above the clouds into the great blue sky. Sunlight reflected off the metallic wings that diverted the air creating lift. Louise thought, *From this height I can almost sense the curvature of the earth.*

During the flight Louise and Sadie chatted incessantly. They were surprised when Sonny's voice came over the speaker: "Ladies, we're making our final approach into Chicago's Municipal Airport and will be landing in about twenty minutes. We may experience some wind and turbulence; but don't worry, this old gal can take it."

Louise gazed out the window at the partially frozen lake and felt a chill despite the warmth inside the cabin. Undeterred by the wind, Sonny stuck an excellent landing.

After they taxied to the gate and exited the airplane, Sonny handed Louise a card from the Hotel St. Claire on 162 East Ontario Street. He said, "Ladies, here's some money to grab a taxi out front. Your room is reserved, so check in with the front desk for your key. I have to refuel, do a maintenance check, and secure the plane. I'll meet you at high noon for lunch in the hotel restaurant."

Louise gave Sonny a kiss on his cheek. "Great job flying. We felt totally safe with you in control." Louise thought, *Why can't I love this man? He's perfect!*

He looked into her eyes—wanting to devour her. Instead, he returned the kiss. "Thanks for the confidence. Next time you'll have to ride up front with me. You won't believe the view from there."

Louise hailed a cab and presented the card. The taxi driver was very informative. "Chicago is world famous for its unique architectural styles from Art Deco to the great cathedrals. The variety is reminiscent of the city's multicultural heritage and history." The driver chatted on until finally he announced, "Ladies, here we are at the Hotel St. Claire."

A bellman ushered them inside to the warmth and elegance of the lobby. Louise and Sadie were escorted to their room on the twelfth floor, where the view was breathtaking. The waves off Lake Michigan were crashing onto the sea wall and freezing—creating interesting ice sculptures.

Sadie asked, "Isn't Chicago fascinating?" Then she quickly added, shrugging her shoulders, "Brrr! I sure wouldn't want to live here."

After unpacking and freshening up, they went to the bar. "Hello, ladies. I'm Big Al your bartender. Name your poison. Where are you two lovelies from?"

"We're from Nashville and we'd like a shot of your finest Tennessee whiskey."

"Good choice, ladies. What brings you two to the frozen icebergs?"

"I'm singing at the Chez Paree for three performances. My name's Louise and this is my good friend Sadie. "

Impressed, he replied, "I'll have to check out your show. You know, a lot of musicians from the South come to this city to make a name for themselves. There are a lot of blues and jazz clubs here in Chicago. You ladies must experience Chicago's night life. There's nothing quite like it."

Right on time, Sonny walked in and Louise introduced him to Big Al. "Kind sir, I would love a Jack Daniel's on the rocks, please," Sonny said. After finishing their drinks, he escorted Louise and Sadie to lunch.

As they were leaving the restaurant, Sonny said, "You ladies have a leisurely afternoon while I take care of some business. Let's meet at the bar at 7:00 p.m. Mike's taking us to dinner, and then we're going to listen to some jazz."

"That sounds lovely. We'll see you then," Louise replied.

Eager to meet the orchestra, Louise made a quick decision to walk a block to the Chez Paree while Sadie chose to hang at the hotel. Several musicians were casually sitting around tuning their instruments when Louise sauntered in with her easy Southern style and introduced herself. The ensemble made her feel very welcome, although rehearsal was not scheduled until the next morning. Everyone was excited to get a head start; so Louise gave them a list of her song selections, and they had a quick run-through. The combination of Louise's vocal talents harmonizing with some of Chicago's finest musicians produced a sweet synergy. As Louise's confidence grew, her memory of Hank receded into the background.

Louise and Sadie strolled into the bar at ten minutes past seven to meet Sonny and noticed he was engrossed in conservation with a handsome man. Upon noticing their approach, both men stood. "Wow! You ladies look amazing. Please allow me to introduce Mike Fritzel, owner of Chez Paree. Mike, this is Louise and her friend Sadie."

Mike extended his hand and replied, "Welcome to Chicago, Louise. I'm happy to meet you, and I'm looking forward to your performance. I heard you've already met the orchestra. That's ambition. And Sadie, nice to meet you too. I'm glad you accompanied Louise." Sadie offered her hand and gave a demure smile in return.

"I'm happy to be here and thrilled to have this opportunity," Louise said, cordially acknowledging Mike.

Sonny piped in. "Ladies, Mike's taking us to dinner and will be our musical tour guide afterwards. He's suggested a quaint but popular place called Café Bohemia over on Clinton Street. They're renowned for their authentic wild game dishes."

After arriving at the charming restaurant, the waiter brought out several courses and placed them on the table family style. They feasted on goose liver pâté and a beet salad with a sweet Thai citrus dressing. For entrees, the waiter presented them with grilled elk medallions and filets of Pike with Louis Sauce.

Sonny looked admiringly at Louise. "It's good to see you laughing and enjoying your dinner."

"The food was divine. I've never tasted anything so delicious," she beamed.

After finishing their five-course meal, Mike said, "Come on, you crazy people, let's go have fun and explore the night life of Chicago."

CHAPTER 25

Adventure in the Wilderness

*H*ank calculated the time it would take for a rescue train to arrive and realized they would have to spend another cold night in the wilderness. Tonight, though, they would be much better prepared.

After digging a shallow hole, Hank placed three layers of coal inside the impression, and then stacked wood on top. He thought, *Once the coal gets hot, it will produce ample radiant heat and will burn for hours.*

An unused piece of sheet metal from one of the hopper cars was placed behind the new fire pit in hopes that it would reflect the heat. Hank washed out the empty bean cans from their dinner the night before and filled them with small pebbles from the stream. Punching holes in the cans, he ran a rope through them, and then wound it around the perimeter of their camp. Hopefully, this would alert them of any uninvited visitors straying too close.

Lucas was still in pain, but thankfully, the bleeding had stopped. Hank got him settled and spent most of the day exploring and scavenging for firewood. It was a cold, brisk day, but the azure blue sky showed no sign of clouds. In the afternoon, Hank whittled a spear out of a young sapling and snagged three large trout in the calm shallows of the river. Trout was a welcome improvement over beans and tough jerky.

The sun was going down behind the mountains—turning the sky into shades of fuchsia and lilac purple. Hank got the fire roaring hot and laid the trout on a flat rock next to the heat. Since the sky was clear, he placed the tarp as a barrier between them and the cold ground. The two, stranded survivors were in much better spirits than the night before. Hank found two pieces of flat, shale rock on which to serve the trout. Lucas ate ravenously and moaned with appreciation as the hot juices ran down his chin.

The stars twinkled lazily overhead in the cold, clear night. They talked for a long while swapping adventure stories. Hank was getting to know Lucas and was becoming rather fond of the young man. He admired his positive attitude.

Finally, Lucas said, "I've got this watch. Why don't you get some sleep?"

"Thanks, Lucas. I'll take you up on that offer. You'd better wake me if you need any help."

Hank snuggled in between the log and the fire and instantly started thinking about Louise. He missed her so much and wished he had a way of delivering a message. The warmth of the fire allowed his body to relax. He let go of the tether to consciousness and drifted away dreaming of finding Louise.

Opening his eyes slowly, Hank noticed that shimmering rays of crimson and golden light were spilling over the purple mountain tops. Lucas was sitting on the log carving something with his knife.

"Why didn't you wake me?" Hank asked.

"You were sleeping so good I didn't want to disturb you. Besides, I couldn't have slept anyway. It was such a perfect night; I was communing with nature. Thank goodness the wolves and the bear left us alone," Lucas answered.

Sleeping on the hard ground had made Hank stiff and sore. He stood up and stretched to relieve his achy body. "Wow! That coal really helped the fire stay hot, didn't it? It sure felt good."

"Yes, it did. Don't bother looking for any food, 'cause we don't have any."

Hank grabbed his handmade spear. "I think I'll go see if I can snag a couple of trout." As he was walking to the stream, he stopped and yelled, "Lucas! Listen! Did you hear that?" Just then a train's whistle blew three long blasts to announce its arrival. Hank started jumping up and down, whooping and hollering and dancing around the fire. Lucas placed two fingers in his mouth and let out a shrill whistle.

Once Hank regained his wits, he scrambled over the rock slide and went running to meet Charlie. Hank embraced him tightly. "I've never been so glad to see anyone. I knew you'd come. We've had quite the wilderness adventure, but I'm ready to go home."

"Are either of you in need of medical attention?" Charlie asked.

"Yes! We were attacked by a pack of wolves, and Lucas got bit pretty bad."

Charlie was shocked. "What? You were attacked by wolves! You two have had quite an adventure."

"Well, that's certainly not the kind of adventure I would sign up for," Hank replied.

The crew was hanging back, so Charlie motioned for one of the men to come over. "Hank, this is Doc Hannity. He's gonna take a look at our boy."

Doc grabbed his bag and made his way to Lucas. He attentively inspected the injury and cleansed it with Mercurochrome and a tincture of iodine. Lucas let out a yelp and started blowing rapidly on the affected area.

"Young man, you've had quite a scare, but everything's gonna be just fine after I stitch you up. Gauging from the size of the wound, I'd say you need at least 30 stitches. Hank could you hold his leg still while I stitch him up?"

Doc got busy and when he finished tying off the last knot, he said, "Son, as soon as you get back to Nashville you must get a series of rabies shots. They're gonna hurt like hell, but we can't take a chance on you getting rabies. Hank, you did a fine job with the first aid. That's a nasty tear. He could have bled out or developed a bad infection."

Lucas said, "Thanks. Doc. Hank saved my life and shot that wolf right between the eyes. He gave me this here fang as a souvenir."

"Son, that's not something I'm particularly proud of. Regardless, everyone needs to know that Lucas has a new nickname. He now goes by *Sir White Fang*."

The rescue crew laughed and cheered. Charlie, being all business said, "All right, everyone, let's get to work clearing this slide. Hank, we've coupled an extra locomotive on our rear so you'll be headed out. An engineer is standing by ready to take you and White Fang back to Nashville pronto."

"Charlie, as always you're the man with a plan."

"I'm just glad y'all are all right. I'll see you back in Nashville. Go home, so we can get some work done. There's some breakfast and hot coffee waiting for y'all in the cab."

Hank looked at Lucas. "What do you say, White Fang, are you ready to get rolling again?"

Lucas grinned big and said, "Let's saddle up, Wolf Slayer."

Hank arrived in Nashville late evening three days before Thanksgiving. He was happy to be home and to see Tallulah, but it was Queenie who gave him the most ambitious welcome.

Tallulah listened intently as Hank told her the story about the landslide, surviving two cold nights in the wilderness, and the wolf attack. He paused for a moment. "That's not the craziest thing that happened on this run, though. Louise was on the southbound train to Thurmond."

"What? She was on the train? Oh! Hank, did you talk with her?"

He was appreciative of the fine whiskey in his hand and took a sip. "Yes, we talked and everything was going well. She even asked me to go to Chicago. Would you believe I told her I couldn't leave my job because the railroad depends on me? Tallulah, I blew it again, but you'll be happy to know that I'm taking your advice."

After he explained his plan, Tallulah looked at Hank with sad eyes. "Hank, darling, I'm so sorry to tell you this, but Louise has already left for Chicago. I stopped by The Noel and inquired about her. Your persnickety little man told me that she had left for Chicago a week earlier than planned."

Hank felt the air go out of him as surely as a balloon deflating. Tallulah cradled Hank's face with her hands and expounded, "Hank, look at me. Don't give up. All is not lost. Louise will be back in less than three weeks. It's not over!" She continued, "Perhaps this will cheer you up. I'm cooking Thanksgiving dinner. Charlie will be back by then, and we'll have a big feast."

"Thanks, Tallulah, you're always the optimist. I love that about you. All right, I'm gonna pick my heart up off the floor and go take a shower."

"Good! That's the Hank I know."

On Thanksgiving day, Tallulah and the railroad cowboys were seated around the table. Charlie put a second helping of sage dressing and candied yams on his plate. "So, Hank, tell me about your adventure in the wilderness and the saga with the wolf attack."

Hank forked another piece of roasted turkey and cranberry sauce. "Perhaps that's a story to be shared with an after-dinner drink by the fire. Right now, all I'm thinking about is this delicious feast. Thanks, Tallulah, for all your time and effort creating this tasty spread."

"Once again, we gather to celebrate life and the harvest. The real bounty is not what lies before us but the gratitude that lies within us. My heart overflows with love. We've so much to be thankful for. Happy Thanksgiving!" Everyone lifted their glasses in celebration of Tallulah's toast.

They were just finishing a piece of German chocolate cake when the phone rang. Tallulah answered, and then handed the receiver to her brother. She whispered, "It's Mr. Johnson." Standing close by she could tell by the look on Charlie's face that it was not good news.

He hung up the phone—choking back tears. "A freight train has crashed through the Shoals Creek Bridge and all aboard were killed. The bridge collapsed on them. They never had a chance. The victims' names won't be released until police have notified the families."

They were all stunned into silence. Charlie continued, "Hank, you were right about that bridge. I wrote in my report about its unstable condition and suggested that a crew be sent out for inspection. They never did a damn thing. Now it's too late. I guess they didn't want to shut down the tracks and lose revenue."

Hank closed his eyes thinking, *That could have happened while Louise and I were on the train.* Then he looked at Charlie. "With every crossing of that unstable structure, I cringed. I felt like it wasn't a matter of if the bridge would collapse but when."

Tallulah silently said a prayer of gratitude that her cowboys were home safely.

CHAPTER 26

Death Rides the Rails

*L*ouise stepped into a black Cadillac Limousine with Sonny and Sadie for the short trip to the Chez Paree. As they turned the corner onto Fairbanks Court, she saw her name in the marquee lights. She let out a small gasp, and her hand quickly covered her mouth in disbelief. Louise felt the illusion that time stood still just for a moment. The limo then turned into the alley and stopped by the private stage entrance.

The Chez Paree was the most elaborate and sophisticated night club in Chicago. Their wealthy clientele ranged from politicians and famous actors to gangsters. Tonight was no exception. Mayor Edward J. Kelly had a prominent table up front with his entourage, and they were eager to hear the new singer.

As the lights dimmed, a hush came over the room, and then the curtain slowly rose. Louise stood beside a grand piano, wearing her favorite green velvet gown. She felt immersed in the passionate bliss of the moment as excitement coursed through her veins. Louise intended to seduce her audience and make them forget about their troubles for a while. The drums started with a soft roll, and then the horns punched in. "Sweet Home Chicago" was her first number, and the crowd went wild. From the sentimental delivery of love songs, to the bump and grind of jazzy tunes, the crowd was rocking. They loved her. After her final number, Louise bowed and the audience applauded loudly as she exited the stage. Waiting in her dressing room was the largest bouquet of roses she had ever seen along with a chilled bottle of champagne, compliments of Sonny.

Mike had arranged for a late-night dinner celebration at the world-famous Green Door Tavern where he raised his flute for a toast. "Louise, you were fantastic tonight. My heart is as full as my glass as I drink to you."

A spontaneous feeling of pride and gratitude swelled within Louise. "Mike, tonight was more than I could ever have dreamed of. I'm so beyond delighted."

It was getting late when Louise finished her delectable dinner. Fatigue seemed to steal her energy. Sonny took notice and offered to accompany her back to the hotel. She gladly accepted. Mike volunteered to escort Sadie to an after-hours jazz club for a night cap.

"I'm just next door if you want to talk," Sonny said. She inserted the key into her door and left him with a smile.

Louise stepped out of her warm bath and slipped into a fuzzy robe. She was preparing for a much deserved night's rest.

Suddenly she remembered that Sonny and Sadie were leaving the next morning. A cold loneliness seeped into her heart. The thought of being in Chicago by herself became unbearable. Louise thought, *When will my lonely heart learn its lesson?*

Without stopping to think, she knocked on Sonny's door. He opened it with a smile. "I was hoping to see you again tonight."

"Sonny, let's not pretend," Louise said as her robe slid onto the floor. He immediately embraced her and kissed her tenderly before slipping out of his own clothes. Without speaking, they lay flesh to flesh, feeling each other's needs. His hands slid beneath her derriere—drawing her closer. Louise arched upward and felt him enter her. With each thrust she sensed herself dissolve in an ocean of pleasure. Their bodies were slick with perspiration as they climaxed together— escaping into ecstasy.

Afterwards, lying in each other's arms, Louise felt hot tears escape down her flushed cheek.

Sonny sensed her unease. "Sweetheart, what's wrong?"

"Tomorrow you're leaving and I'll be alone in this frozen tundra for Thanksgiving. Forgive me, I don't like being negative. Please don't think that I'm not grateful. It's just that ever since my family died, holidays always make me feel melancholy. Don't you worry, though. I'll be fine."

Sonny held her tight. "Sweetheart, you know I would stay with you if possible, but I have important business that can't wait."

It would be nice if for once I were the most important business on someone's agenda, she thought.

Louise donned her robe and kissed Sonny on the cheek. "I'm going to my room before Sadie comes back. Please forgive me if I don't say goodbye. It just sounds so final, so I'll see you later in Nashville." She closed the door and left him with a sad smile.

Early morning came and Sadie was feeling the effects of too much fun and alcohol. Louise ordered room service and helped her pack. Afterwards, Sadie gave Louise a warm embrace and left to meet Sonny for their return journey home. Louise sat in a wing-backed chair gazing out the window at the frozen lake. Sonny's departure had left her feeling as fragile as a torn butterfly's wing.

Louise spent Thanksgiving alone—grateful for a day of rest. She struggled with conflicting feelings about Sonny and her regrets and sadness over Hank. Sleep was her escape.

The day after Thanksgiving, Louise was enjoying breakfast in her room, feeling well rested and looking forward to another rehearsal day. She poured herself a cup of coffee that was blended with subtle hints of citrus and rich chocolate. Taking another appreciative sip, she picked up a copy of *The Chicago Tribune*. While perusing some interesting articles, a shocking headline caught her eye.

Death Rides the Rails

Yesterday a Louisville & Nashville freight train headed towards Nashville, Tennessee, from Thurmond, West Virginia, fell over two-hundred feet to its demise when the Shoal Creek Bridge collapsed. The wooden trestle and truss bridge was originally built in the early 1800s. Authorities are investigating the incident. There is controversy regarding violations of weight restrictions and other safety precautions.

The only eyewitness, a local fly fisherman, reported a graphic description as the bridge splintered and disintegrated. His statement referred to the explosion as sounding like a bomb had exploded. The coal cars became uncoupled, flipped and tumbled, smashing into the rocks and into the rapid current of Shoal Creek. The witness divulged briefly hearing horrifying screams as over one-hundred hopper cars filled with coal crashed and piled on top of the locomotive. Fire erupted from the twisted wreckage. Due to high winds the flames spread rapidly, turning the pileup and surrounding area into an inferno. The smell of burning was gut wrenching.

There were no survivors. The names of victims will not be released until the families have been notified.

Louise panicked, as she remembered what Hank had said about that bridge. Tears blinded her eyes. She lost her breath. The thought that Hank could possibly have been on that train was more than she could bare. *Hank, I'm so sorry for the way I left you. I pray that you are safe. I just hope I have another chance to tell you how much I still love you.* Louise was pacing the floor, crying and not knowing what to do. With high anxiety, she picked up the phone and had the operator dial Sonny on his private line. When he answered she started sobbing uncontrollably, feeling as though she were emotionally sabotaged.

All Sonny understood was train wreck. "Sweetheart, stop and take a deep breath. You've got to calm yourself. I've heard about the wreck, but the railroad isn't releasing any information until next of kin have been notified."

"Sonny, you have to get me home now. I have to find out about Hank."

"Let me talk with Mike," he replied. "I'll see if he'll release you temporarily from your contract. Unfortunately, the weather is too bad to fly, so I can't come get you. I'll make arrangements for you to board the next southbound train. In the meantime, get packed and try to remain calm. I'll be back in touch as soon as I have your itinerary."

After Sonny hung up, he released a heavy sigh. From the sound of Louise's frantic voice, it was clear that she was still in love with Hank. Even though he knew his chances with her were illusory, he sincerely hoped that Hank was not involved in the fatal train crash.

The phone rang and Louise rushed to answer it. Sonny's voice was reassuring. "Hi, Sweetheart. Unfortunately, I haven't heard any new information regarding the train wreck. The good news is, under the circumstances, Mike has generously released you from your contract. You can return in the spring for another engagement. There's a car waiting in front of the hotel to whisk you to the train station. Try to relax and think positive. I'll be waiting when you arrive in Nashville."

"Sonny, thank you for taking such good care of me," she tenderly replied.

Louise boarded the train and cuddled with a warm blanket in her cabin. It wasn't the cold she was trying to dispel; it was the fear in her heart. The possibility of losing Hank was paralyzing. With misty eyes, she thought, *If I'm fortunate enough to be given another chance, I'll never let that man out of my sight again. My pride and ego will not hold me back from saying the things my heart is yearning to say.* All Louise could do was try to remain optimistic and ride the rails back home, far away from the frigid icebergs.

CHAPTER 27

Black Friday

*H*ank and Charlie arrived half-an-hour early for the mandatory employees' meeting per Mr. Johnson's request. He invited them into his office and closed the door. "You are two of my most dependable men. I'm promoting you both to a supervisory position on this recovery project. Charlie, you're my head man for organization and logistics of this operation. You have great managerial skills, and it's time to put them to use." Mr. Johnson sipped his hot coffee and continued. "Hank, I realize you haven't been here that long, but you've illustrated exemplary work ethics. I'm putting you in charge of site planning, preparation, and evaluation. Those mountains will present some obstacles, no doubt, but I believe you'll make informed decisions. You're also in charge of maintaining the trains and supervising the loading and unloading of supplies and equipment. Work closely with the bridge engineer and give him what he needs. He's the boss in charge of this construction project. You'll both be generously compensated for your time and inconvenience. Any questions?"

"No, sir, you've been pretty thorough. We're ready. Let's roll," Charlie replied. Hank nodded in agreement.

At 8:00 a.m. sharp, Mr. Johnson walked to the podium. "Good morning, everyone. This is indeed a Black Friday. As you already know, a terrible tragedy has occurred. I apologize, but I'm not at liberty to release the names of the deceased until next of kin have been notified. Our heartfelt sympathy goes to all their families and to our lost crew members. Let's take a moment of silence to honor our fallen men." When the room became uncomfortably quiet, Mr. Johnson continued: "Their loss will be felt for many years to come. The reality is we're faced with a massive challenge. All traffic has ceased operation since the bridge collapsed. A lightning fast response is required to get the trains rolling again. We need to quell the situation, clean up the site, and recover any and all damaged materials to be shipped and sold as scrap. Firefighters are still working hard to contain the flames." Mr. Johnson paused as if trying to regain his momentum. He wiped the sweat off his brow and continued. " I have chosen a bridge contractor, and the plan is to build a temporary trestle bridge to open the tracks. Once this is in place, steel and stone will be transported to the site to reinforce and replace parts of the trestle. This will result in a safer and more permanent structure. We are going to need every able-bodied man on site, so be prepared and pack a bag. You'll be leaving just as soon as the train is loaded. There will be supervisors instructing the operation on every level. We have crews from the north and south ready and on standby. This way the project can be accessed from both sides of the bridge. Men, this is going to be a long and tedious recovery. Our main objective is getting that bridge up and operational. A tent camp will be set up for your accommodations; cots and blankets will be provided. Be sure to bring warm clothing and extra pairs of socks. Thank you, men. I appreciate your courage and loyalty. Let's get those trains rolling."

The cowboys drove home and shared the news with Tallulah. She helped them pack warm clothes and extra socks as suggested. The leftover Thanksgiving meal was packed in a box along with the remainder of the German chocolate cake.

"Sis, I don't know when we'll be back. It'll probably be at least a couple of weeks if not longer. I'll try to get word to you. Take care of yourself and don't worry about us. We've got Hank here to keep us straight."

A sleeper and dining car had been added behind the engine for the crews' accommodations. Mr. Johnson wanted them fresh upon arrival—ready to hit the ground running. Darkness had fallen, and nothing was visible outside the windows except for an occasional lonely light that sparkled on the landscape. Charlie and Hank spread out the Thanksgiving feast and were thankful for Tallulah and the food before them. After finishing their supper, they ravaged the delicious cake.

"Damn, that was good cake. Hey! This is nice. I could get used to being a passenger on a train," Charlie commented.

Hank chuckled and replied, "Difference is, you ain't going on no vacation."

The next day they arrived at the scene of the accident and spoke with the lead investigator, who handed Hank a list with the names of the victims. Hank gasped and his knees almost buckled when he read the name, Lucas Gray. "Oh! No! Not Lucas! Not White Fang. He was so young and full of life."

Charlie threw his arm around Hank, and they just stood there in silence trying to comprehend the horrible loss many would soon feel. Charlie cleared his throat, choking back the tears as he gazed at the devastation. He surmised that upon impact the engine burst open, spilling its hot coals. The rapid combustion along with the dry tinder in the area had started a brush fire in the canyon. The fire had been contained, yet there were still cinders floating into the air and smoke billowed from the charred wreckage.

As Charlie and Hank took inventory of the surroundings, they could not believe the surreal scene before them. The one-hundred ton locomotive had nosedived into Shoal Creek and was partly submerged. The freight and hopper cars were crumpled like matchsticks—some with their wheels facing skyward and some with no wheels at all. Their eyes simply could not grasp the carnage they were witnessing.

Snapping back to reality, Charlie took control. "Ok, Boys, we've got lots of work to do. Let's prioritize from high to low what needs immediate attention. I'm going to work on a plan to get organized and set up schedules. We'll stake out the best site for the camp, as that should be our first priority. The camp needs to be up and operational before the next wave of workers come."

Due to the elevation and uneven terrain, Hank realized they were going to need ramps to unload all the equipment. Hank delegated a crew to start clearing a site for the camp. Then he took measurements, and with regard to weight bearing, started designing ramps. They would have to be built on site—a daunting task, but not impossible.

Their mission: to build a bridge and get the wheels back on the steel.

CHAPTER 28

Next of Kin

Louise arrived at Union Station and Sonny was patiently waiting on the platform. She ran to him. "Sonny, I'm grateful to you for getting me back. Would you mind waiting just a bit while I check in with the trainmaster? I'm just worried sick about Hank. I have to know if he was on that train."

"Sure, no worries. I'll be waiting at the bar inside. Welcome home, by the way."

Louise walked with purpose to the trainmaster's office and barged in without even knocking.

"Excuse me, Sir. I'm inquiring if Hank O'Neill was on the train that crashed."

"I'm sorry, ma'am, but I'm not authorized to give you that information until next of kin have been notified," Mr. Johnson replied exasperated.

"I'm Louise, Hank's wife. Is that kin enough for you? Now please tell me, was my husband on that train or not?"

"It's nice to meet you. I'm Mr. Johnson, please have a seat. I'm happy to inform you that Hank was not on that train. He's not here, though; he's working as one of my supervisors on the recovery project. You should be proud of Hank. He's one of my best employees."

Louise grabbed the chair and literally fell into it as relief washed over her. "Oh! Thank goodness my prayers have been answered. I'm so relieved but sorry for the families who have lost loved ones. When will Hank be returning?"

"This is a massive project and we need all available men on site. Our project manager is working on a schedule to rotate the men every two weeks, but we'll just have to wait and see how it goes. Stop back by in a couple of days, and I'll have more information for you."

"Thank you, Mr. Johnson. I apologize for the way I barged into your office. I've been in Chicago and the not knowing was making me crazy. Is there any way I can get a letter to Hank?"

"It's all right. I can only imagine the concern you've been through. If you can have a letter here by 7:00 a.m., I'll make sure that my engineer personally delivers it to Hank. We have a supply train leaving for the site at eight a.m."

Louise walked into the bar where Sonny was patiently waiting. He immediately knew that Hank was not on the train as evidenced by the big smile on her face.

A sigh of relief washed over him. Louise sat down beside Sonny and ordered a whiskey.

"Must be good news," he said.

"Yes, good news. Hank wasn't on the train, but he's working at the site as a supervisor. I'm not sure when he'll be back."

"First let me say how happy I am about Hank. Finish your drink. I'll get you back to the hotel, so you can relax from your long journey."

On the way to the hotel, Louise approached Sonny with an idea. "Sonny, what do you think about my doing a benefit concert as a fundraiser for the poor people living in the coal-mining towns of West Virginia? They have so little and suffer so much. I would love to do something to help those unfortunate people. They need food, blankets, coats, shoes, and medical supplies. The children are in bad need of school supplies. What do you think?"

"You have such a generous heart, Louise. I think that's a splendid idea. Let me talk with Cody and see what he thinks."

Back in her room at The Noel, Louise sat down with a grateful heart and wrote a letter to Hank.

My Darling, Hank,

While in Chicago I read a newspaper article about the train disaster. You cannot imagine the fear that racked my body. The possibility of your being on that train brought such agony. I cancelled my tour and left on the next southbound train. In the sleepless hours of the night, my heart was filled with such anxiety, but I held on to the hope that you were alive and well. Upon arriving in Nashville, I spoke with Mr. Johnson, and he informed me you were not on the wrecked train. Relief washed over me. Hank, the thought of living in this world without you is inconceivable. Please accept my apology for the way things ended when last we met. If you will give me another chance, I promise to make it up to you. I made a vow to myself that when I get my hands on you again, I'll never let you go. Even though there has been such an abyss of space and time between us, I've never stopped loving you. I love you more than ever, and to know that you still love me means everything to me. My heart is a burning flame that aches for you, and my body is simply crazy from wanting you. Please come back home to me.

Your loving wife,
Louise

The following morning, Louise dropped the letter to Mr. Johnson and decided to visit Sadie.

"Louise, what a surprise. You're back from Chicago," Sadie said.

"Yes. When I read about the train crash, I just had to cancel my tour and return home to find out what I could about Hank. Thankfully, he was not onboard the train, but he's working at the crash site. I don't know when he'll be back. It took something dramatic to make me realize how madly in love I still am with that man. He's my life and my happiness is to be near him."

"That's such good news, Louise. I've been sick with worry ever since I heard about the crash. By the way, I have some interesting news to share. It seems that Calvin and Carmen are totally smitten with each other. Their planning a trip to Costa Rica. We even discussed the possibility of my buying her boutique."

"How interesting that meeting Calvin on the train not only changed my life, but Carmen's as well. I'm genuinely so happy for them."

As Louise walked back to the hotel, she took special notice of the Christmas decorations. Fragrant evergreen wreaths filled with holly and star tinsels lined the streets. Ribbons and delightful ornaments adorned the downtown shop windows creating a festive mood. Louise walked into The Noel lobby and Mr. Persnickety stopped her.

"Eh! Excuse me, Mrs. O'Neill. I have a note here for you."

Feeling somewhat confused, Louise took the note, ripped it opened, and silently read;

Dear Louise,

Please meet me in the hotel bar this afternoon at 5:00 p.m. I have some important information to share with you. Hope to see you then.

Cordially,
Tallulah Leigh

Louise's jealousy flashed for a moment, but curiosity got the better of her. She arrived at the bar a few minutes early, hoping to dispel her nerves with a proper drink.

Tallulah walked up to the bar—an image of confidence. "Hi! Louise, I'm Tallulah. It's a pleasure to meet you. Hank has told me wonderful things about you. That man is insanely in love with you."

"Hank has also told me about you. Forgive me if I'm not Miss Congeniality. I'm still trying to wrap my head around the fact that you slept with my husband," Louise sarcastically replied.

Pausing for a moment to order a glass of red wine, Tallulah gave Louise's jealousy time to chill. "Hank said you were direct and straight to the point. I can appreciate that. Yes, we did sleep together once. If it makes you feel better, I'm the one who made the advances. I was missing my husband really bad, and Hank was going through a difficult time trying to locate you. He was in a lot of pain, and I selfishly took advantage of the situation."

Tallulah paused again, letting her confession give Louise more assurance. "Hank apologized to me later, but I reminded him that he should not feel guilty, because he was the one left behind. So, if you want to be angry with me, then go ahead; but's that's not the reason I'm here."

Taking a sip of wine, Tallulah stared at Louise, waiting for a reaction. When none came, she continued. "Hank and my brother Charlie will be back in Nashville in a week for a three-day break before they head back out. I would love for you to be my mystery dinner guest the night they return. It would mean so much to me, and Hank will be blown away. Louise, I would love for us to be friends. Please say yes!"

Louise was flabbergasted at Tallulah's compassion and honesty. "Tallulah, you're a stunning woman, and I can see why Hank couldn't resist you. My answer is yes. I am humbled by your grace. Please forgive me. I'm afraid my mind has been filled with the poison of suspicion and jealousy. Tallulah, I can't thank you enough for doing this."

Louise and Tallulah had just left the bar when Sonny sashayed through the brass and glass door in a confident and casual manner. "Well, hello, Louise, and how are you this evening?" he said, smiling.

"I'm fine, thanks. Sonny, please meet my friend Tallulah."

His eyes betrayed him, as he smiled at her admiringly. "So nice to meet you, Tallulah. I do hope to see you again soon." Then turning to Louise he said, "I thought you would like to know that Cody has said yes to your benefit concert. We'll talk tomorrow. Good evening, Ladies."

Tallulah was intrigued with the man that walked away. She asked, "Who was that?"

Louise answered, "Oh! That is a very long story."

CHAPTER 29

Fast Approaching Storm

Hank had cleared the land and the workers' camp was up and operational. Most importantly, two latrines had been installed downwind. The bridge construction was making considerable progress. Several short spans were completed—each supported by the trestle frames beneath. The trestles created a strong frame in the form of a tripod to keep the track solid and safe high above the ground. Laborers were working the structure from both banks to eventually meet in the middle. Another crew worked primarily on dismantling, salvaging, and removing the wreckage to be hauled from the site as scrap. An environmental crew would follow with the cleanup. The project was challenging, but the men were feeling optimistic. They were looking forward to the next shipment of food and supplies.

Sam Jenkins was retiring from the railroad after thirty years of service. His nickname, "Sweet Daddy," was due to his insatiable appetite for sweets and women. This run delivering supplies to the crash site was to be his last trip as engineer. As was his habit on long runs, Sweet Daddy packed his briar-wood billiard pipe with his favorite English-blend tobacco. He loved the aroma, and the first draw was like heaven. Sliding the cabin window open, he exhaled a big puff of aromatic smoke. Sweet Daddy then leaned out the window to do a visual safety check of the trailing cars. Unfortunately, the wind was too strong and the letter that he was delivering was sucked right out of his breast pocket. He briefly saw the letter flying through the air before it disappeared into the landscape.

As the hours and miles passed by, Sweet Daddy became more bothered over the incident. He had always prided himself as being professional, yet now his lack of competence upset him.

Eventually, he arrived at the crash site as a man with a worried mind. Finding Hank busy unloading a heavy piece of equipment, Sweet Daddy cautiously approached. With his head hanging low, he said, "Excuse me, Hank! I need to speak with you." Hank turned off the ignition and jumped down from the bulldozer. He took off his cap and scratched his head as Sweet Daddy continued. "Mr. Johnson asked me to deliver an important letter to you, but unfortunately it flew out the cab window. Hank, I've failed you and I just feel terrible."

"Don't beat yourself up," Hank said kindly. "I'll be returning to Nashville soon, and I'll find out about it then."

While surveying the site, Sweet Daddy thought, *I must say that I'm really impressed with this operation.* Then sadly, he said, "Hank, that kid, Lucas—he volunteered to cover a shift for someone. He shouldn't have been on that train. It's such a shame. He was so young. I heard the story about how he became known as White Fang. You must have been rather fond of the boy."

Putting his arm around the old man's shoulder, Hank replied, "Yes, Lucas was a great, young man. His loss is such a tragedy. We're all still grieving."

Changing the subject, Sweet Daddy's voice became alarmed. "Hey! I don't know if y'all have heard, but there's a big snowstorm headed this way. It should be here in a couple of days. It's gonna be a bad one. If need be, I can help y'all evacuate."

"No, we haven't heard any news here," Hank replied. "I'll certainly talk it over with Charlie and see what he has to say. Go on up to the mess tent and grab yourself some food."

Hank found Charlie disciplining a worker over some infringement. Charlie ran a tight ship and would not tolerate anyone breaking the rules. Getting his attention, Hank said, "Hey, Charlie. I need to talk with you." Hank motioned him to the sleeper car, where they could talk in private. "Sweet Daddy just informed me that there's a bugger of a snowstorm headed our way. Should we shut down the project and evacuate?"

"This is certainly not good news. Management won't be happy, but we can't expect these men to survive a massive storm in a tent. Hank, start the evacuation announcement, and I'll try and get a telegraph to Nashville."

Charlie radioed the engineer on the south side of the bridge with instructions for him to send a telegraph from Thurmond to Union Station. The message read:

SHUTTING DOWN OPERATION. STOP. FAST-APPROACHING STORM. STOP. HAVE ORDERED AN EVACUATION. STOP. WILL RESTART PROJECT WHEN FEASIBLE. END MESSAGE.

The engineer answered, "Will do. Charlie, this is a fast approaching storm. We need to get out of here asap. We're starting evacuations as well." Charlie felt good about his decision and knew it was the right thing to do.

Tools and equipment were secured as the workmen prepared the site for evacuation. Finally, all preparations were complete and the work crew was safely on board. As they were leaving, Hank stuck his head out the cab window and gazed at the eerie sight. A large cross cast a silhouette across the landscape. The men had fashioned it out of twisted metal from the wreckage as an altar to honor the dead. Hank felt his heart sink as he choked back tears—sadly saying goodbye to his young friend, White Fang.

Hank and Charlie arrived at Tallulah's the next afternoon. She was so surprised. "I'm happy to see y'all, but I wasn't expecting you 'til next week. Did something happen?" Charlie hugged his sister and explained their situation. She nodded in understanding and said, "Why don't y'all take a shower and a nap? You must be exhausted. I need to go to the grocery store. I'll wake y'all when supper's ready."

On her way to the grocery store she stopped at The Noel and asked for Louise. While waiting in the lobby, Tallulah was absorbed in memories of her rendezvous with Louise at the bar; but what she really remembered was the way Sonny had smiled at her.

Louise walked up and jolted her back to reality. "Hey, girl, looks like you were deep in thought about something."

"Oh! Sorry. The guys are back in town. They had to shut down the operation due to a big snowstorm. They were exhausted, so their probably taking a nap now. Why don't you come with me and join us for supper? Hank will be so surprised."

Louise felt her heart leap in her chest. Happiness streaked through her like a shooting star. Her delight unfolded like a wild flower blooming from a spring rain. "Wow! This sure is exciting news. Look at me, I'm trembling. The pain of my separation from Hank has been such a test, but it's nothing compared to the joy I'm feeling right now. No amount of space and time can separate you from the one you're meant to be with. What's meant to be will always find its way. My most humble gratitude to you, Tallulah"

CHAPTER 30

Happy Day

$\mathcal{L}$ ouise crossed the threshold into Tallulah's charming cottage and immediately felt at ease. She thought, *The energy in this home feels positive— like love lives here.* Awakened from her nap, Queenie came bounding into the room to greet their guest.

"What a gorgeous dog," Louise commented as she petted her playfully.

"Thanks! Queenie was my husband's dog, but she's definitely mine now. She's been a great comfort to me."

"Hank told me about your husband's untimely passing. My sincere condolences. I know how I felt at the thought of Hank being on the train that crashed. I can't imagine the pain you've been through."

"Life is for the living. Even though I miss him terribly, I had to find a way to keep going. Moving to Nashville has really helped."

Louise gave her a sympathetic smile, and then looked out the window towards the carriage house. *So this is where Hank has been all this time,* she surmised. Dark thoughts entered her mind as she ruminated about Hank making love to Tallulah. *I must meet the present moment with an openness and not keep reacting to these negative emotions.*

When dinner was ready, Tallulah whispered to Louise, "Go hide in my bedroom. In about fifteen minutes, slip outside and knock on the front door. I'm going to round up the guys for supper."

Louise was feeling a bit mischievous, so she knocked loudly on the door three times. Wham! Wham! Wham! Charlie jumped up from the table in a defensive mode. "Who the hell is that banging on the front door?"

"Sit down, Charlie, and relax. I'll get the door," Tallulah ordered. She answered the door, but didn't open it all the way so that the guys could not see who was there. They stood in the doorway talking in low, hushed voices, trying to build suspense. Tallulah realized that Charlie was becoming curious, so she escorted Louise inside.

Hank had just taken a swallow of his drink when he looked up to see Louise smiling as she casually strolled into the house. He was so surprised that he spewed sweet tea across the table. His eyes got wide and he became aware of his own heartbeat fluttering in his chest like a flock of seagulls. Jumping up from the table, Hank ran to Louise and threw his arms around her so tightly that she could hardly breathe. He released their embrace and held her face tenderly. Looking into her hazel eyes, Hank said, "Louise, I can't believe that you're really here. Damn, woman, how I've missed you. I'm so sorry for the way things ended with us on the train. Darling, I promise I'll never put anything before you again."

Louise smiled from ear to ear. "Shhh! My darling! Don't you worry about that. Hank O'Neill, you're mine, and I'm never letting you go." Tallulah and Charlie were on their feet whistling and applauding loudly.

"Hello, Louise, I'm Charlie. Welcome! We're so glad that you're here. You have no idea how Hank has longed for you. This is a happy day indeed."

They laughed and shared stories while having supper. Louise explained how Tallulah had left a note for them to meet. "When I saw Hank on the train, he confessed his encounter with Tallulah. So, at first I wasn't exactly friendly until she told me about her plan to invite me over for dinner. Hank, you were right. I now understand what an amazing woman Tallulah is."

Charlie looked at his sister with a question mark on his face. Louise felt foolish as she realized he had not known about their liaison. An awkward silence fell over the table.

Tallulah was gracious and quickly recovered. "Yes, Hank and I had a weak moment one night, but I knew he was still madly in love with Louise."

Hank spoke up, "Tallulah, you have been so wonderful to me. I can't thank you enough for bringing my Louise home. Supper was delicious. The company was great; but we have some urgent business to attend to. Goodnight all."

Everyone broke into laughter. After the lovers left, Charlie looked at Tallulah suspiciously. "Sis, you are just full of surprises now, aren't you?"

Tallulah just smiled and replied, "Yes, I am."

✳

As Hank and Louise walked to the carriage house, she said, "Oh! Hank, we've so much to catch up on."

"There will be plenty of time for talking later. Come inside, woman, I'm going to ravish every inch of you." They closed the door on the world. Hank took his time undressing her. He placed her slender fingers to his lips kissing each one tenderly. Closing her eyes, she felt the readiness between her thighs. It felt as though an electric current coursed her entire body. Hank's lips came down on hers with a savage hunger. His hands were following the curves of her beautiful breasts down to her shapely hips. They lay face to face, touching and caressing, getting to know each other again. Hank reached between her thighs and slipped a finger into her wetness. Louise's body seemed to hum with the wonder of his touch—awakening the memory of them. Louise felt herself dissolve into a pool of undenied pleasure. Then he took her—all of her. She felt her body explode with satisfaction as her hips became unhinged.

He whispered. "This is where I belong." Hank and Louise made sweet love long into the night. After their passion was spent, the lovers slept in each other's arms as moonbeams cast enigmatic shadows across their bed.

Early morning light was creeping through the windows, and Hank awoke aroused. He inhaled the scent of her hair and kissed Louise gently on the neck. She slowly came back to life, moaning from the sheer pleasure of being next to her man.

She nibbled on his earlobe and whispered, "Did you get my letter?"

"Oh! The letter was from you! No, I never got it. Unfortunately, the engineer lost it on the trip down."

Louise fluffed her pillows making herself more comfortable. "Hank, there was an article in a Chicago newspaper about the train wreck. When I read about it, I almost lost my mind thinking that you could have been on that train. I remember your mentioning concerns over the bridge being unsafe. I cancelled my show and was on the first train headed to Nashville."

"Louise, my darling. You're back in my arms and that's all that matters. Except, right now, I have some pressing business to take care of. Damn woman, I can't get enough of you."

The sun was shining brightly when they entered Tallulah's cottage and smelled the aroma of coffee percolating. Queenie was feeling frisky and came running to Hank for some loving.

"Good morning, love birds. Have a seat. Breakfast is almost ready. I was thinking we could have a tree trimming party tonight to celebrate," Tallulah said while flipping the bacon. "We need to get into the holiday spirit. Charlie, could you find us a beautiful tree today?"

"Sure, Sis, but only if you'll make your famous hot-buttered rum."

Tallulah teased, "What would the holiday season be without it?"

Louise picked up the newspaper and perused the want-ads until she came across something in the real estate section that grabbed her attention.

> *Eighteen-Hundred's Farm House—Foreclosure*
> *This charming old home sits on seventy-two*
> *beautiful acres with rolling hills just twenty minutes*
> *outside of Nashville. A picturesque stream*
> *flows into a large bass-stocked lake.*
> *Virgin timber towers over the landscape.*
> *For more information or to view property,*
> *Call Lillian Blevins JE8-6440*

Excited, Louise almost shouted, "Hank, take a look at this ad. Can we go look at this property? It sounds amazing."

He read the ad, and then kissed Louise on the cheek. "Why not? I've been saving my money and dreaming of the day we could have a place of our own. Let's see if we can look at it today."

"I have an appointment with Sonny and Cody later this morning to discuss the logistics of a benefit concert for the coal miners and their families. I haven't had a chance to tell you, but you're welcome to come sit in on the meeting if you like.

Hank was happy to comply. "I'll call the realtor, but you go ahead with your business meeting. I'll wait and hear the details from you later."

Charlie offered Louise a ride downtown, since he was heading out to run some errands.

After Charlie and Louise left, Hank looked at Tallulah with a mischievous grin. "Hey! I could really use your help in finding the perfect diamond ring for Louise."

CHAPTER 31

Magic of Romance

$\mathcal{L}$ouise was giddy. The meeting with Sonny and Cody had gone extremely well. The benefit concert was scheduled for December 19 at The Noel. After Cody left Louise remained seated. She paused, trying to find the right words to tell Sonny about Hank. He gave her an empathetic smile and said, "Louise, there's no need for an explanation. When you called from Chicago, I knew that you were still in love with Hank. As much as it hurts to say, I'm sincerely happy for both of you."

"Thank you for being so understanding. Sonny, you've been so good to me. I'll never forget that."

Afterwards an uncomfortable silence filled the room. Wanting to shift their attention, she gave him a coy smile. "Sonny, we're having a tree-trimming party tonight. Why don't you come?" Then she teasingly said, "Tallulah will be there."

"Well, yes. I could do that. Since you broke my heart, it's the least you could do. Is Hank going to be good with this?"

"Yes, Hank knows. He also knows how much you've helped me. He will be fine with meeting you."

Sonny lit a cigar and was blowing smoke rings toward the ceiling like he was deep in thought. Louise decided to be daring. "You're a very handsome man and quite the catch. I can't help but wonder why you don't have someone special in your life."

"My wife, Linda, died two years ago after suffering terribly from a rare form of cancer. For a long while I didn't think I could go on. Death leaves such a heartache that takes time to heal. Thanks to you, this cold and lonely heart of mine has unthawed a bit."

"Sonny, I'm so sad to hear about the loss of your wife. I sensed a pain deep within you that you carry silently. Linda's memory will always be a part of who you are, but I'm glad you've opened yourself to love again. It takes courage to keep living and loving. I found out recently that Tallulah's husband was killed in an accident a short time ago. She still bears the scars of her loss as well."

Louise wrote down Tallulah's address. "I look forward to seeing you tonight." They hugged as friends—who were once lovers. Louise left him feeling great about where her life was headed. She hurried to invite Sadie to the party. Tallulah agreed with Louise that Charlie needed to meet someone fun and interesting.

Hank's head was swimming. Mr. Roberts, the jeweler, was passionately explaining the intricate details of diamond rings. "The circle of the ring symbolizes infinity and never-ending love. The first decision in buying a diamond is to select the cut, then choose the color and grade."

As the jeweler droned on, Hank noticed a very whimsical ring in the display case, and asked Tallulah what she thought of it.

"Oh! Hank. That ring is so unique. I've never seen anything like it. If you're looking for something special, then this is the one."

Mr. Roberts smiled. "Good choice. That ring is an Irish design called the "Entwined Celtic Love Knot." The band is made of rose gold and the knot is of white gold. The ring is accented by a one-carat, heart-shaped diamond. An inscription inside the band, *From My Heart To Yours*, makes for a romantic motif."

Hank failed to ask the price; the Celtic design had sold him. He and Tallulah walked out of the store with a gift wrapped box. Hank was beaming, *Finally, I'm going to present Louise with her very own wedding ring.*

Tallulah was fast approaching a Ford dealership, when Hank asked, "Would you mind stopping so I can look at the pick-up trucks?" She pulled in and told Hank to take his time while she dashed across the street to get cinnamon sticks for the hot-buttered rum. Hank walked into the showroom and noticed that the new 1937 models were on display. A personable salesman approached and introduced himself as Will Clinton. "Can I help you, sir?"

"My name's Hank, and I'm looking for a good deal on a pick-up truck."

Will pulled on his long, white beard and steered Hank to the lot. "The best deals will be on the 1936 models. We have two left. I could give you the most off of sticker price on this crimson one over here. It seems that Tennesseans aren't particularly fond of that color."

Hank laughed. "I like red. Could you hold this truck 'til tomorrow? I would like to bring my wife to look at it. We'll have more time to talk then."

"Sure, but isn't that your wife who just drove up?"

Playfully Hank quipped, "Naw! She's just my girlfriend."

After everyone returned to the house, they were greeted with the divine aroma of venison roast and veggies that had been slow-cooking since early morning.

Louise turned on the radio to tunes from Bing Crosby's Christmas album. Hank retrieved the decorations from the attic, while Tallulah prepared the hot-buttered rum. Charlie came in dragging a nine-foot Christmas tree behind him. There was a festive mood in the air that was contagious. While the hot-buttered rum was being passed around, the doorbell rang.

Mumbling quizzically, Tallulah said, "Louise would you get the door? That must be Sadie, 'cause I'm not expecting anyone."

The door was opened to reveal Sadie and Sonny, both arriving at the same time. Louise welcomed them and introductions were made.

Tallulah approached Sonny with a calm pleasantry that she hoped masked her racing heart and offered him a mug. He accepted it, while making certain that he slightly touched her hand.

"I hope you don't mind that I crashed your party," Sonny teased.

"You're a nice surprise," Tallulah beamed. "I guess I have Louise to thank for this. I'm delighted you're here."

Concealing a pang of jealousy at seeing Sonny, Hank nonetheless walked over and shook his hand. "Nice to meet you, Sonny. I'm Hank." Pleased by Sonny's calm demeanor, Hank continued, " I understand you're a pilot." At that remark, they started a comfortable conservation about trains and planes.

Tallulah announced that supper was ready. The gentlemen pulled out chairs to the right to seat the lady next to them. Tallulah dinged her glass, calling attention to her announcement.

"Before we eat, let's feel the love and gratitude in our hearts. Love is a universal gift to the generous heart. Breathing love into a thought brings inner balance, and gratitude brings us to a place of appreciation that allows our souls to fly free. I'm so grateful for my life and you, my friends, for sharing it. This is a happy holiday season indeed."

After supper Tallulah filled her guests' mugs and invited everyone to join in decorating the perfectly-shaped cedar. "What Will Santa Claus Say?" by Louis Prima and His New Orleans Gang was playing when Sonny asked Tallulah to dance. He guided her gracefully beneath the mistletoe and gazed into her emerald eyes that punctuated her glowing skin. He felt as though the ground shifted beneath his feet. Sonny kissed her gently on the cheek. She smiled and subtly pulled away on the pretense of attending to the decoration of the tree.

The crackling sounds of fire and happy holiday music filled the room, along with peals of laughter. The smell of cinnamon and fresh pine from the Christmas tree permeated the space. The magic of romance was thick in the air, like wisps of lingering smoke.

Even Sadie and Charlie, an unlikely pair, were having a good time. Hank pulled Louise in closer to him and whispered into her ear. "This, my love, is all because of you. I don't think I've ever been happier in my entire life."

CHAPTER 32

Rolling Waters

*H*ank rolled over to snuggle with Louise but discovered the bed empty. His mouth felt about as dry as an empty creek bed from all the rum he had drunk. When his eyes finally focused, he noticed a light in the adjoining room. He wrapped a blanket around his naked body and walked into the small sitting area. There sat Louise with pen and pad scribbling away hurriedly.

Hank kissed the top of her head and then plopped down beside her. "Darling, what are you doing up so early? It's barely daylight."

"Oh! Hank! I've had this song in my head for days, and it just had to come out. It still needs work, but please tell me what you think."

He picked up her hastily scribbled verses and started to read.

Bring Back The Sunshine And Roses
Roses that grew in love's garden wilt since you've gone away
Hours that we knew among the flowers are only dreams today
Bring back the sunshine and roses,
Let's live once again days of old,
Bring back your smile
That made life worthwhile
Your charms that my arms used to hold
Bring back the blue to the sky dear, you took when you went away
Bring back the sunshine and roses when you return some day

Birds in the trees have quit their singing
I miss their sweet refrain
They seem to know
I miss you so and want you back again
Bring back the sunshine and roses
Let's live once again days of old
Bring back your smile
That make my life worthwhile
Your charms that my arms used to hold
Bring back the blue to the sky dear
You took when you went away
Bring back the sunshine and roses when you return some day

"Darling, this is good. I love it! Let me grab my guitar, and we'll put it to music."

"We've got plenty of time for that. Let's go back to bed. I'm cold." They snuggled under the covers and started chatting about everything from buying a truck to the dynamics of the party.

Hank kissed Louise on the neck before saying, "I know how you must have felt meeting Tallulah, because it was strange for me to meet Sonny. I have to admit that I like him, though. It seems rather uncanny that he and Tallulah have taken a liking to each other. You wouldn't have had anything to do with that now, would you, my darling?" Louise moaned with pleasure as Hank massaged her neck and shoulders.

"I just gave Mother Nature the coordinates; she took her own direction." Louise laughed. "Yes, this is weirder than words can describe and the irony isn't lost on me. You have to admit, though, it's all so strangely beautiful. Let's get our butts into the kitchen and prepare breakfast. I'm starving."

The smell of coffee and bacon frying aroused Tallulah and Charlie. They came stumbling out of their bedrooms like zombies.

Charlie said, "Last night was a blast, Sis. Louise, thanks for inviting Sadie. She's quite a gal. Hank, Mr. Johnson has scheduled us to work at the yard until we can get back to the site. We're to report in Monday morning."

"Sure thing. Charlie, would you mind dropping me and Louise off at the Ford dealership? We just might be buying a truck today. Then we want to take a look at that farm."

Louise started clearing the table, and without hesitation she asked Tallulah, "Did I detect some romantic sparks between you and Sonny last night?"

"That was a nice surprise, thank you. I don't know where, if anywhere, our friendship will go. Sonny is intriguing, and the possibility of being with someone whose company I enjoy is enticing. He did ask me out for dinner, so stay tuned."

Negotiations for the pick-up truck were finalized. She was a beauty with a curvaceous, chrome grille, skirted fenders, a laid-back windshield, and a three-speed manual transmission with 85 horses under the hood.

Before leaving, Louise had to mess with the salesman in her usual playful manner. She looked at him sternly and asked, "Will, was my husband in here yesterday with another woman? You had best tell me the truth." The look on Will's face was priceless. He was speechless.

Hank let Will stew for a minute, then said, "Will, she's just messing with you, man. That other woman's a good friend of ours."

"Man, I felt like I was on the guillotine and the blade was ready to drop. Louise, you sure had me going there for a minute," Will said after laughing heartily.

Hank and Louise drove east on a curvy two-lane blacktop, leaving the city behind. The rolling hills and peaceful valleys of the countryside stretched out before them. Christmas music was playing on the radio, and Louise was singing along. She paused and said, "I love you, Hank O'Neill, but I really love our new truck."

Hank said laughing and reached over for her hand. "I love you too, woman. Scoot that pretty butt of yours over here next to me."

Louise held the piece of paper tightly with the directions to the farmhouse that the realtor had given them. Hank hit the brakes almost missing the entrance to the gravel driveway. An ancient iron gate with ivy-covered stone columns in need of repair greeted them. A very old, rusted metal plaque announcing "Rolling Waters" was barely visible through the vines. Hank got out of the truck and unwrapped the chain that held the gates together. Just beyond the gate was a bridge over a picturesque flowing stream.

"Hank, I've got chill bumps. This place is amazing. Just listen to the water gurgling over the rocks."

Pushing in the clutch, Hank shifted into first gear, and they slowly rolled across the bridge and down the winding drive. He paid special attention to all the virgin timber on the land. When the farmhouse became visible, Louise released a gasp. Sitting on a hilltop overlooking a serene and peaceful lake stood an abandoned and mysterious-looking house that was aged from the environment and neglect. Immediately after getting out of the truck, Hank started appraising the integrity of the house. Louise noticed that what once was a beautiful rose garden was now overgrown brambles and weeds. Paint was peeling off the walls, and the shutters were barely hanging on their hinges. Tangles of poison oak vines crept up the brick chimney. The filthy windows dully reflected the blue sky. "This place needs lots of work, but the house seems to structurally have good bones," Hank said.

A spacious porch wrapped completely around the house. The charming dormer windows seemed to look down on them with hopeful eyes. Dental molding accented the eves and roof line. Whoever built this house certainly spared no expense when it came to details. It was obvious even through the neglect, that this house once had its glory days.

"I love this place. It feels like the home I've always dreamed of," Louise said as she ran to Hank and grabbed his strong hand.

The front door was stuck and Hank struggled to open it. With one last run and a shoulder push, the door flew open and creaked on its hinges. Hank bowed, took Louise by the hand, and escorted her across the threshold. Greeting them was a forsaken old piano sitting in the living room amid an array of Federal-styled windows. Louise gasped as her slender fingers ran down the untuned keys, producing an eerie sound that echoed off the walls.

"This piano was probably too heavy and expensive to move," Hank surmised.

Throughout the house, dust and cobwebs created a haunting scenario. Rubbish was everywhere, and the windows were thick with grime. A musty smell permeated the interior from being closed up for so long. For a brief moment, Louise thought she smelled roses, then she laughed at that ridiculous thought.

As expected, Hank began to take rough measurements and notes so that he would be prepared to make an offer on the house. Ideas were flowing through Louise's head, and all she could manage to do was clasp her hands and whirl with glee thinking, *I'm going to have so much fun breathing life back into this space.*

A cool breeze embraced the newly-joined couple as they strolled down to the reflective lake. Louise took notice of the ancient willow tree that graced the bank with its cascading foliage. Having grown up with a willow tree in her front yard, Louise had created her own symbolism for the tree. *Adjust to life, adapt to changes, be graceful, and bend but don't break.*

"Hank, are you ready to take on a project of this magnitude?"

He squeezed her slender hand. "I think of all the reasons why and why not—I don't see any of the latter. I can just see you with our kids playing in the yard."

Pausing briefly to reflect before making a final decision, Hank said with determination. "Let's do it! It's gonna take a lot of work, but I can't think of a better investment of our time, energy and money."

"Hank O'Neill, you have made me the happiest woman in the world."

"Darling, let's go back to town and talk with the realtor. Why don't you drive? This is your truck too."

Louise had been watching Hank intently to learn the mechanics of driving. Eagerly, she scooted into the driver's seat, pushed in the clutch, and turned on the ignition. Hank knew he was in trouble. Shifting into first gear, she popped the clutch and hit the gas. Louise took off careening down the driveway spinning gravel and smiling like a wild banshee.

As Hank held on for dear life, he just looked at her and grinned. "Louise, you are one wild woman, but could you please slow these horses down a bit?"

CHAPTER 33

Wings of Destiny

Hank and Louise came to a successful negotiation with the realtor. They signed the contract for their new home located at 560 Palmer Road. Before the ink was even dry, Louise grabbed Hank's hand, barely able to conceal her delight. A joy greater than she had ever known was unearthed inside her. Hank was smiling profusely as happiness resonated through him. There were no words for the love and gratitude that filled their hearts.

Louise slid behind the wheel, and they sped home to share the good news. She fumbled to find the windshield wipers as snow started dropping softly. A light layer of accumulation lay silently upon the ground. Louise pushed the clutch in and down-shifted the throaty engine into first gear before turning into their driveway. Charlie and Tallulah rushed outside to admire the new truck. Hank and Charlie were talking excitedly as they admired the engine underneath the hood. Louise and Tallulah quickly grew bored and left them for the warmth of house.

Tallulah stoked up the fire as Hank and Louise's voices rose passionately while talking about purchasing their dream home and the months of remodeling ahead.

Hank suggested, "The Juke Joint over on Granny Smith Road has live music tonight. I'm hungry. Anyone up for some BBQ and blues?"

It was Saturday night, and the bluesy sound of Big Bill Broonzy was resonating off the walls. Hank looked around the table and smiled at his good fortune.

"Hank, wipe that silly grin off your face," Charlie said.

"Brother, see this face? This is true happiness right here."

Late in the night, as predicted, the snow turned into a chilly, soaking rain. Sunday morning came calling as soft shadows and a mysterious mist hung in the dripping woods. Hank and Louise were tangled in each other's arms. Hank nuzzled against her neck and whispered. "What kind of spell have you put on me witchy woman? I'm totally and hopelessly forever in love with you."

She gave a wicked laugh and said: "By fire and earth, by water and air, so you be bound to my desires."

⚘

Monday morning Louise met Sonny at his office. He greeted her enthusiastically. "Good news! We have changed the venue for the concert because The Noel is too small to accomplish our goal. I contacted The Ryman, and even with short notice they were able to work it out. They have more seating, and the acoustics are much better. Louise, this is your destiny—your star journey."

"Wow! The Ryman—that's intimidating but amazing nonetheless."

Aware that Louise was new to Nashville, Sonny shared some history. "The Ryman was built in 1892 by a river boat captain named Tom Ryman. It's called *The Carnegie Hall of the South.*"

"That's interesting. Speaking of destiny, Tallulah has a book of famous quotes and this one by William Jennings Bryant resonated with me: *Destiny is not a matter of chance, it's a matter of choice; it is not a thing to be waited for, it is a thing to be achieved.*"

"When we record your debut album, what if we call it *Wings of Destiny?*" Sonny jotted the title down on a notepad before continuing, "I want to say thanks for introducing me to Tallulah. I'm just crazy about her, but we've decided to take it slow. I also enjoyed meeting Hank. You've got a good man there, Louise."

"Wings of Destiny? I like it. Yes. I do have a good man. Sometimes you have to get hit in the head with a brick before you realize the truth right in front of your eyes."

⚘

Saturday night the Ryman Auditorium was flooded to the rafters with people. The lights went down and Louise was introduced. She stepped from the shadows and walked confidently onto the stage, wearing a sleek and sensuous cobalt blue gown accented with flowing ivory silk and a string of pearls. She took the mic and smiled at her audience.

"Good evening, ladies and gentlemen. It's an honor to be on this stage. I would like to thank our talented musicians who have kindly donated their time for this endeavor. Thank you all for coming tonight to support this benefit. The proceeds from tonight's concert will go to help the impoverished coal miners and their families in West Virginia. Many of you may not know that my husband, Hank, and I were once one of those families. These people are barely surviving and are in need of even the most basic necessities. As soon as the new bridge is completed, we will have a shipment ready for them. If anyone would like to volunteer to help in our effort, you may sign up in the lobby. Thanks to all of you for being a part of something bigger than yourself. Let's share a little holiday cheer and a lot of love for our coal-mining neighbors. Engage with us and let's enjoy this evening of giving."

Louise started singing "At The Christmas Ball," a Bessie Smith tune. She then picked up the tempo with "The Fairy On The Christmas Tree." She sang a few more holiday songs and a couple of original tunes slated for her upcoming album. For the finale, she had decided on the happy upbeat song, "Jingle Bells" written in 1857 by James Lord Pierpont. As Louise triumphantly sang the last note, the entire audience stood whistling and applauding loudly. She took a final bow, and before gracefully exiting the stage, she looked directly at Hank, who was beaming. Louise threw him a bundle of mistletoe wrapped in red ribbons. Inside was a note that said: *I love you, Hank, heart and soul.*

CHAPTER 34

Irony and Mystery

ouise donned her heavy coat and went outside to crank the truck and let the engine warm. Her breath exhaled fog from the cold, winter morning. Hank and Charlie piled into the cab and Queenie jumped into the truck bed. After dropping the men off at the depot, Louise headed to rehearsal. The railroad cowboys were working hard at the yard organizing the next trip back to the bridge site.

After rehearsal Louise decided to do a little Christmas shopping, while Queenie waited patiently in the front seat. She wanted to buy Hank a railroad pocket watch, because his father's old watch failed to keep time properly. Curiosity caused her to sashay into a pawn shop where she inquired about watches.

An elderly man, with a tobacco-stained chin said, "Purty lady, today's yo lucky day. I have right here a Hamilton Elinvar 992 railroad pocket watch. See, it's engraved with a locomotive on da back. That redwood burl dial and crystal is in purfect condition. Hamilton Railroad is there on tha crown, see that? It's a real nice watch and it works mighty fine. I'd let you have it for say twenty dollars."

"Say, it's not worth a penny over ten dollars. That's my final offer," Louise countered.

"Sorry, Ma'am, I can't let it go that cheap. That right thar is a expensive watch."

Louise had started for the door when he called her back. "All right, all right, I'll take ten. You drive a hard bargain, little lady. How did you learn to negotiate like a man?"

Slapping ten dollars on the counter, Louise grabbed the watch and case. She looked directly into his eyes. "It may come as a surprise to you, but women have brains, too. In life you don't get what you deserve, you get what you negotiate."

While strolling down the street, Louise felt rather proud of her negotiating skills, but she was more excited about finding the perfect watch for Hank. About a block down the street she noticed a jeweler and decided to have the watch personally engraved *From My Heart To Yours, Love Louise 1936* on the inside of the case. While walking back to the truck, she started musing about how much her life had changed. She flashed back to the image of herself sitting on the bench anxiously waiting for the train to Nashville. Then she remembered her grandmother's words, *If you have courage and faith in yourself, then you have the power to manifest the life you want. Fear and doubt are paralyzing and lead to becoming a victim.*

Louise had a few hours until she had to pick up Hank and Charlie. With a quick decision, she sped towards their recently-acquired farmhouse. She loved driving the truck. Hitting the blacktop offered such a sense of freedom. Besides, she could drive faster when Hank was not with her. While driving past each fence post, it seemed that all the pain and hardships she had endured left her like shingles flying off a house in a storm. Happiness enveloped her in a warm blanket. She smiled and pushed the pedal just a little harder.

Tallulah had a book on Feng Shui that Louise had read and found intriguing. The book explained how to use energy forces to harmonize individuals with their surrounding environment. She studied how to cleanse the residual energy of a space before applying the principals of Feng Shui. No doubt the history of their old farmhouse harbored secrets, and the past needed to be cleared with a thorough cleansing. These thoughts were going through Louise's mind as she slowly ascended the creaky stairs. Light was streaming through the stained glass windows, casting eerie shadows across the central staircase. Suddenly she heard what sounded like a little girl sobbing. Louise was startled. She immediately stopped and listened to a haunting echo of violin music, along with a shuffling of receding footsteps. Queenie's hackles went up and she started growling.

Queenie's presence comforted Louise and gave her courage. "Who's there?" No one answered. She stood like a statue on the stairs and listened intently, but no other sound came. Louise thought, *Perhaps it's my imagination playing tricks, but why would Queenie have growled if she hadn't sensed something too?*

On high alert, Louise cautiously continued up the stairs. As she walked into the bedroom on the right, she felt a cold shudder trickle down her spine. The air was bitter cold. After each chilly inhale she exhaled steam. *The temperature in this bedroom is definitely colder than the rest of the house*, she thought. A warning of goose bumps covered her body. Louise caught a whiff of roses. *How strange! That's the same scent I smelled before.*

An uneasy feeling ran through her veins as she continued to explore. Even though the upstairs rooms were uninhabited, it felt as though someone was watching her every move. With trepidation, Louise climbed the creaky stairs towards the attic. She forcefully opened the stuck door and a musty and stale odor assaulted her. Beside the door, an old, metal bracket supported a kerosene lamp and a box of matches. Both were covered in dust. The lamp oil had mostly dehydrated, but there was enough residual to produce a soft glow. The lighting in the attic was diffused and eerie. Cobwebs and spiderwebs were suspended from the roughhewn, rafter beams. She heard something scurry away and then noticed evidence of vermin droppings. Looking around the room, Louise observed a very old rifle leaning in a corner next to an ax. Sitting on the floor was a mantle clock with a frozen face ineffectually staring back at her. Then her attention landed on an ancient, wooden box. Curious, she opened it to find a cache of old, faded photographs. As she quickly perused through them, one particular photo of a rather stern-looking couple captured her imagination. The woman was holding a small girl, who looked to be about six or seven-years-old. A violin rested in the child's lap. On the back of the photo was the faded and scribbled names of Jake, Sarah, and Adelia Rose. Louise stuck the photo into her jacket pocket and wondered if that small family were the ones who had lived in this once luxurious home. Louise thought, *I'm going downtown to the Institute of Historical Archives and research the history of this old farmhouse. Something strange must have happened here.*

Queenie started barking and ran down the stairs and found Tallulah at the front door. Louise descended the creaky stairs and decided not to mention her unusual encounter in the attic.

After observing the natural beauty and tranquility of the farm, Tallulah then walked inside the cold house and marveled at the architecture. Louise had brought a thermos of hot coffee and offered some to Tallulah. As they sat on the stairs drinking coffee and shivering, Louise said, "I'm glad you decided to come check out the old place; but, before I show you around, I want to hear about your date with Sonny.

Tallulah took a sip of the hot brew and smiled bashfully. "Sonny is one of the most romantic men I've ever met. He took me to a cave that stays the same temperature year-round. When we walked into the first chamber, there was a circle of candles blazing. The reflections dancing off the crystals were mesmerizing. A blanket with pillows and a picnic basket was spread within the circle under what looked like a chandelier of crystals. We could hear water dripping into a pool in the distance. Sonny laid out a beautiful lunch with smoked salmon and opened a bottle of champagne. We talked for hours. It was absolutely perfect. I'm afraid there's no hope, I'm falling madly in love with him."

"I'm so happy for the two of you. I know it's hard to let your heart trust again, but I believe Sonny is an honest and sincere man. Our lives are filled with such irony and mystery. Maybe one day I'll write a song about that."

"Our lives are like a strand of pearls with each pearl telling a different chapter of our life. For example: if you hadn't left Hank, you and I would never have become friends."

Louise shivered and pulled her jacket tighter. "We're gonna need some whiskey to continue this deep conservation. I've got to go pick up the cowboys from work. To be continued..."

"I would be happy to come with you tomorrow and help you clean," Tallulah offered.

"Thanks, I would love that. First, I must warn you that I suspect this house is haunted. I could really use your help in cleansing this space."

"Haunted? Now that adds another dimension. So, let's create another intriguing chapter to our already exciting story."

Louise added, "One pearl at a time."

CHAPTER 35

Embracing the Smudging

$\mathcal{L}$ouise and Tallulah went into the Institute of Historical Archives to research the history of the farmhouse. With help from a friendly clerk, they quickly located information on Rolling Waters.

Jake and Sarah Rose built the farmhouse in 1815. Jake was a wealthy, shipping tycoon from the East Coast and spared no expense on the construction. Adelia, the couples' only daughter, had contracted scarlet fever and died in the house at the age of six. Jake and Sarah abandoned the farm and moved back to New York City. After several years of neglect, the State took possession of the house and property. The clerk informed them that the house was sold to a Smith family from Georgia about twenty-five years ago. They were the last known people to live at Rolling Waters. The Smiths fled because they claimed to be experiencing paranormal events. Rumors circulated throughout the area that the house was haunted. The property had remained vacant ever since.

"Is this incredible? A little girl is still haunting the place where she died over a hundred years ago. We need to help Adelia's spirit pass into the light," Louise said as she looked at Tallulah in disbelief.

"That sweet girl. It must have been horrible for her. Adelia is stuck in this dimension and needs our help."

Louise lit a fire, and when smoke started roiling back into the farmhouse, she hurriedly opened the damper. Tallulah could not help but laugh because Louise's face was covered with soot. When the flames were blazing high, they started burning all the old articles of clothing, papers, and junk that were strewn around. Louise and Tallulah worked hard, and by noon they had the downstairs cleaned, as well as the filthy windows. The place was starting to shine, and Louise was loving it. Her imagination was on fire, thinking about paint colors and such. She had started an idea file from past issues of *Better Homes & Gardens* magazine.

Before any of that could happen, electricity and heating needed to be installed, along with a pump for the well. It was going to be an involved project, but Hank and Louise were excited about the renovation.

While sitting in front of the fireplace enjoying their ham sandwiches, Louise and Tallulah heard a sobbing sound resonate throughout the house.

"Did you hear that? Oh my goodness," Tallulah exclaimed.

"Yes, the first time I heard her it shocked me too. We need to do a space clearing right now. I brought a plethora of tools. Are you ready for this?"

"Yes! Not only is it important to help Adelia, but this needs to happen so that you and Hank can claim your space."

Louise arranged a decorative, silk scarf in front of the fireplace. On it she placed the following: a sage stick in an abalone shell, candles representing the four cardinal directions, a small bowl of pink salt, a large crystal, and a Tibetan bell. She then positioned the photo of the Rose family in the center of the altar. Tallulah opened the front and back doors and all the windows that were not stuck to allow the stagnant energy in the room to escape. They both sat cross-legged in front of the altar and took deep breaths to clear their minds. Louise lit the sage stick, and a cool breeze blew through the house embracing the smudging. Tallulah lit the candles while stating her intentions. Sage smoke was wafting throughout the room when the candles suddenly went out and the front and back doors slammed shut simultaneously. The harrowing sound of a screeching violin reverberated throughout the space. They about jumped out of their skin, but were resolved to continue the ceremony.

Louise leaned over and whispered to Tallulah, "I think someone is having a temper tantrum." With authority, she relit the candles and Tallulah reopened both doors. Together, they strolled through each room. Louise sprayed a mixture of water, fresh rosemary, and orange peel. Tallulah cast salt as she rang a bell.

In a resounding voice Louise spoke, "Adelia, I'm so sorry for what happened to you as a beautiful young girl. That was so unfair. Please know that we are here with love in our hearts to help you move on to where you belong. This is not your home anymore, but a better one awaits you. Your parents are there. Don't you want to see them again? They miss you so much."

Beautiful violin music sounded serenely in the background, and the smell of roses became very prevalent in the room. Louise continued, "Adelia, sweetheart, it's time to let go and move on to the light. I promise to keep your memory alive and will always respect this place that was once your home. Rolling Waters is now my home, and I humbly ask that you respect that." A mournful silence settled over the house.

Louise and Tallulah returned to the altar and sat for a moment in meditation. Louise rang the bell, and the third time it rang pure and clear. They opened their eyes and witnessed a mirage likened to a heat shimmer rise and quickly dissipate. A tranquil feeling descended upon the space.

Tallulah whispered, "Adelia Rose has moved on."

Smiling in agreement Louise then recited an old Celtic House Blessing: *"Wishing you always walls for the wind, and a roof for the rain. Hot tea beside the fire, and the love and laughter of those you hold dear. May this home be a sanctuary of love and peace for all those who shall enter here. I do hereby claim this space."*

The two friends embraced—overcome with emotions. Louise beamed and thought, Now the renovations can begin.

CHAPTER 36

Romantic Rendezvous

$\mathcal{H}$ank contrived a plan to present Louise with her long overdue wedding ring on Christmas Eve. On December 23 Charlie drove him to the farmhouse, so he could discreetly prepare for a romantic rendezvous. After entering the house, they noticed that the space felt different, lighter perhaps. Fresh garland and holly were hung over the front door and the fireplace. Two, red candles were placed on the mantel. Hank had borrowed a rug and two old straight-back chairs from Tallulah's storage shed and positioned them carefully in front of the hearth. He cleaned out the ashes and strategically stacked kindling and wood into the fireplace. A strike of a match was all that was needed to enjoy a nice fire.

On Christmas Eve, Hank asked Louise if she would like to take a ride to the farmhouse to watch a winter sunset. Never one to miss a sunset, she eagerly agreed. As they were bouncing down the highway, she reiterated her experience with Adelia. "It's very strange, but I felt so connected to that little girl."

"I understand. That's how I felt with Boxcar Billy and Night Rider. I never used to believe in ghosts. We would be arrogant if we denied the possibility that another dimension exists. Life is one big mystery, but I'm happy just to be here with you."

Hank parked in front of the house, and Louise immediately noticed the garland on the front door. "Santa's little elves have been here, I see."

"Take a walk down to the lake and have a seat on the blanket I've laid out. I'll join you shortly." Hank suggested.

"Oh! Mystery man, what do you have in store for me?"

"Just you wait and see," he said smiling from ear to ear.

He walked inside the house and lit the fire and candles before joining Louise. The placid lake was reflecting glorious colors from the sunset. He kissed Louise on the cheek and gave her the gift-wrapped box. Surprised, she tore through the paper and ribbon—gasping when she saw the brilliance of the flawless ring. He slipped it on her finger and knelt down looking lovingly into her eyes: "Louise, you are my equal in all things, and this is my sacred vow to you. I promise to love, respect, and care for you all the days of my life. I vow to nurture your dreams, because through them your soul shines bright. If we live in truth and trust, there's nothing we can't face. May we grow old together and have many adventures to tell our grandkids. My love, this heart is entirely yours, and I solemnly promise to always put you first above all else."

"Hank, I'm speechless. What a wonderful surprise. This ring is exquisite. Tell me about it. It's the most precious gift I've ever received."

"It's not near as precious as you, my darling. I've always wanted to buy you a ring—even though I could never afford one. When I saw this ring I knew it was made for you. It's called The Entwined Celtic Love Knot, and there's an inscription inside the band—*From My Heart To Yours.*"

Louise was astonished at the synchronicity of the phrase, but quickly recovered so as not to reveal her own surprise. She wrapped her arms around Hank and kissed him passionately.

When they came up for air, he said, "Damn, woman, I want you so bad right now, but it's just too damn cold. Let's go inside by the fire and celebrate with some good whiskey."

She had noticed the fire's glow reflecting on the windowpanes and eagerly agreed.

As they sat in front of the fire sipping the smooth whiskey, Louise said, "Well, I have a surprise of my own." She handed him a gift-wrapped package and he clumsily fumbled with the wrapping. Success! He opened the gift and whistled in disbelief.

"Woman, I can't even believe this. Louise, this is the most attractive watch I've ever seen. I will treasure it forever, and someday I'll pass it down as an heirloom."

"Open it, there's an engraving on the inside," Louise instructed.

"This is inconceivable! What are the chances we would both chose the same engraving?"

They sat together in front of the fire enjoying each other's company and reveling in their love.

The fire had burned low and a coldness started seeping into the house. Hank said, "It's getting late and we don't have any more firewood or a warm bed. We'd better go or else I'm gonna ravage you right now on this cold, hard floor."

Louise awoke early Christmas morning and looked out the window. Snow was falling gently on the landscape. The cedar trees were covered in a white blanket—creating a dreamscape. She snuggled next to Hank under the warm covers and whispered, "Merry Christmas, darling. It's snowing outside." He pulled her closer and they cuddled for a long while until sleep claimed them once again.

Later, Hank and Charlie were chatting in front of the fire while sipping on eggnog and whiskey. "I Told Santa Claus To Bring Me You" by Bernie Cummins and His Orchestra was playing on the phonograph. Louise and Tallulah were in the kitchen finishing preparations for a Christmas feast. The table was beautifully set and candles were lit. Tallulah answered a knock on the door with a big smile and greeted Sonny. "Merry Christmas, my love."

The girls disappeared to freshen up a bit before gathering everyone to the table. When they returned, Tallulah picked up a knife and dinged her glass: "Everyone, please take a seat at the table. Our Christmas feast is served. We're sad that Sadie can't be here with us, but she's with her family for Christmas. Before we eat I would like to share an old Irish toast: *A Christmas Wish—May you never forget what is worth remembering or remember what is best forgotten.* Here's to making lots of memories not to be forgotten."

Sonny clapped and said, "Here Here! I have a toast from Sir Walter Scott: *Heap on more wood—the wind is chill. But let it whistle as it will. We'll keep our Christmas merry still.*"

Louise replied with a toast by J.H. Fairweather: *"Christmas"...A day when cheer and gladness blend. When heart meets heart, And friend meets friend.*"

After enjoying their Christmas feast, everyone gathered together in the living room. Sonny presented Tallulah with a card. Inside was a pair of South Sea pearl earrings along with a note that read:

Tallulah,

I would be honored if you would accompany me on a trip to Costa Rica to visit Calvin and Carmen. Love Sonny

Tallulah exclaimed, "Oh! My! Yes! Sandy beaches and warm tropical weather sounds like a delightful reprieve from this cold, dreary December. When are we leaving?"

"I was hoping you would say that. I'm working on the arrangements now to leave within a few weeks," Sonny answered.

Ripping paper was the prominent sound in the room. When all the presents had been unwrapped, Queenie joined in the celebration by rolling around joyfully in the discarded ribbons and papers. Tallulah casually reached inside the Christmas tree for a card that was hidden behind a branch and handed it to Louise. Opening it, she discovered one of Tallulah's pretty handmade Christmas cards. On the cover was a charcoal drawing of Hank and Louise standing by the red truck with Queenie. Louise opened the card and read it out loud:

My Dearest Hank and Louise: I can't begin to tell you both what your friendship means to me. To show my appreciation, I've had Queenie bred with another pedigree German Shepherd. I'd love for you two to have the pick of the litter. Now you can have a dog of your own. Merry Christmas! Love, Tallulah.

Hank was petting Queenie and said, "I thought you were getting a little chunky, old girl. Tallulah, besides Louise and my watch, this is the best present ever."

"What an amazing gift, Tallulah, thank you," Louise added.

"Y'all are so welcome. Anyone interested in a slice of that bourbon-infused chocolate pecan pie?"

Tallulah threw another log on the crackling fire to dispel the chill and lit a few candles. "Santa Claus That's Me" by Vernon Dalhart was playing when Louise said, "I've about had my fill with Christmas music. Anyone interested in listening to some country music?"

"Country sounds good, but Louise, would you and Hank mind giving us a preview of your new song about sunshine and roses? I'd love to hear it," Sonny asked.

They glanced at each other and nodded in agreement. Hank tuned his guitar, and Louise started singing the lyrics to her beautiful love song as twilight descended upon this unforgettable Christmas day.

CHAPTER 37

Sensory Connection

*L*ouise's new album was coming along nicely. Due to the Electrical Age of recording, the fidelity of songs were greatly improved. Sound was captured, amplified, filtered and balanced electronically. It was a true collaboration as Sonny and Louise worked tirelessly on the arrangements of each song, making sure the selection of instruments was correct. One day Sonny said, "Louise, I enjoy working with you. You're a singer, who not only has a musical sense, but knows how to use your instrument to bring life to the song."

A Western Union telegraph arrived one evening for Louise.

GOOD PROGRESS ON BRIDGE. STOP. MUST STAY ANOTHER STINT. STOP. LOVE AND MISS YOU HANK. STOP. END OF MESSAGE.

Regardless of the weather, there was intense pressure to get the bridge operational. Tons of coal were piling up and needed to be transported throughout the country. While Hank was working at the bridge site, Louise spent her time recording and overseeing the renovation of their farmhouse. It was ambitious work, but she was pleased with how things were advancing.

On the last day of January, Sonny flew his plane to New Orleans, where he and Tallulah boarded *The Oratava* at the Julia Street Wharf. Their final port of call was Punta Limon, Costa Rica. *The Oratava* was a freight and passenger steamer ship in United Fruit's Great White Fleet. Although the ships were originally intended for transporting bananas, United Fruit discovered that they could increase their profit margin by adding well-appointed state rooms for adventurous travelers.

While Tallulah was getting settled in their cabin, Sonny made his way to the wheelhouse to meet the captain and crew. His inquisitive mind was fascinated. He asked numerous questions regarding the knowledge required of a river pilot to navigate the challenging Mississippi River.

A Crescent River Port Pilot was in control of the wheelhouse. He introduced himself as Captain J.P. Vogt, Sr. With a voice of authority, he gave the command to cast away the lines. Then he ordered the attending tugboat to go back half and turn the ship southbound. Once the ship was headed south, Captain Vogt commanded the quarter master to steer to a 000 heading. As the vessel approached Algiers Point, he gave the rudder command of starboard 10 to commence their ninety mile trek to the mouth of the mighty Mississippi. The journey continued, and fog began to settle over the river—making visibility an issue. The pilot sounded the ship's horn periodically to gauge the distance to shore and to alert other vessels of their location.

Sonny thanked the captain and pilot and made his way back to the cabin. He found Tallulah pouring two shots of whiskey. "A woman after my own heart." They kissed and then stepped outside by the railing and watched as the world passed by. Sonny pointed out an eerie-looking graveyard, barely visible in the low-lying fog. He wondered about the people who had laid their lives down in the desolate-looking place.

Tallulah looked at Sonny and knew that she was hopelessly in love. She smiled, hardly containing her excitement to be on such a thrilling adventure. Closing her eyes she could already feel the tropical breezes blowing through her long, dark hair.

While Tallulah was away on vacation, Queenie had always greeted Louise with unconditional love. One afternoon there was no such greeting, which was unusual. Concern grew when there was no response to Louise's calls and whistles. She glanced outside and noticed that Queenie was lying in front of the carriage house door. She ran to her and immediately realized there was something seriously wrong. Queenie was whining and in distress.

Louise quickly took her inside and made a warm bed. Water was placed on the stove to boil, towels were gathered, and a pair of rubber gloves were sterilized. Queenie relaxed as Louise petted her and sang an old lullaby. The contractions were becoming harder, and then Queenie's water sac broke. Louise pulled on the sterile gloves and inspected the birth canal, discovering that the first puppy was breech. She thought, *"Lord, I could use some help here. I don't know what I'm doing, but Queenie, we'll figure this out."*
Being very gentle Louise reached her small hand inside and turned the breeched puppy into its proper alignment. Queenie instinctively pushed, and the puppy came sliding out. The new mom licked and cleaned her first baby, removed the mucous so it could breathe, and then helped the pup find her tit.

Queenie laid back down, and Louise stroked her and gave encouraging words. By nightfall, eight, healthy puppies were suckling on their proud mother's warm milk.

After being gone for a month, the cowboys were finally coming home. Louise was ecstatic. She cleaned the house with vigor, took care of Queenie and her puppies, cooked supper, and sang the entire time. Late in the afternoon, she jumped into the truck to go pick up Hank and Charlie at the depot. Louise was so excited to see her man and feel his touch upon her tender skin. She longed to hear his voice teasing her. The long distance between them had not been easy, but the pain of missing him was about to be over.

Louise parked the truck in the employee's parking lot. While getting out of the vehicle, she heard the whistle blow announcing the train's arrival. Filled with anticipation, she made her way towards the receiving track that was adjacent to the main line. Hank's train slowly came chugging into the station. The brakes hissed from the steam being released and the train gradually came to a stop. Hank was leaning out the cab window waving his engineer's hat. His soot covered face could not hide the smile that erupted when he spotted Louise.

"Go to her," Charlie said. "I'll take care of the checklist. Don't worry. I'll catch a ride. I'm going over to Sadie's tonight, so you two can enjoy having the house to yourselves."

Hank swept Louise off her feet and kissed her passionately. "That's just a preview of what's to come, Let's go home, woman. We need to take care of some urgent business."

When they arrived at the carriage house, Queenie started barking and jumping up and down.

"Hank, our girl has something she wants to show you. Don't you, Queenie?"

Queenie escorted him to her playful puppies.

"Oh! My goodness! You've been busy. Which puppy's ours?"

"Meet Duchess. Look at the star on her belly. Even though she was breech, I think the star is a sign of good luck. Isn't she precious?"

"Duchess? I really like that name. By the way, we've got the house to ourselves tonight. Charlie is taking Sadie out for supper."

"That's great. Now get your arse in the shower before we have dinner. By the way, I've prepared a very special dessert for you. It's decadently sweet. It's aroma will make your mouth water. It's warm and moist with a hint of an exotic spice. Warning: before consuming, you must be naked."

After two weeks Sonny and Tallulah returned home sporting healthy, bronze tans. Louise observed that a tan wasn't the only thing Tallulah was sporting. A nice-size rock sparkled on her left hand.

Queenie was excited to show Tallulah her new babies. The pups were rumbling and tackling each other. They were using bouncy movements, initiating play by growling, biting, and lunging at each other.

"They're so stinking cute. Louise, I can't thank you enough for everything you've done. I'm so grateful to you. Have you made your pick?"

Louise handed Duchess to Tallulah and explained the rough delivery Queenie had experienced.

"Ladies, I hate to take my leave, but duty calls. I'm sure you two have a lot of catching up to do anyway," Sonny said on his way out.

"Come sit by the fire. You've got to tell me everything, and I especially want to know about that rock on your finger," Louise said while handing Tallulah a cup of coffee.

"The trip was fantastic. Calvin's coffee plantation, Finca La Puerta del Alma, is absolutely stunning with breathtaking views of the rainforest mountains. We stayed a week with him and Carmen, and then hopped on a small plane and flew to the Osa Peninsula. I never knew such an amazing place existed. Along the beautiful coastline, azure waves crashed down onto sandy beaches with incredible rock formations. Saltwater sprayed into the vast sprawling jungle—creating a mysterious mist. The Osa is a wild and rare place, where wildlife is abundant and crystal-clear rivers empty into the Pacific Ocean. The primordial landscape stirs one's imagination."

"Costa Rica sounds incredible. I'd love to go visit one day. What I really want to hear about is how you got that rock on your finger," Louise anxiously said.

"Well, one afternoon we were strolling on a pristine, deserted beach where huge palm trees reached out towards the sea. The surf was roaring and crashing onto the shore. Gorgeous Scarlett Macaws were flying overhead in pairs, squawking to their mates. We sat down on a felled palm tree to watch an astounding sunset. Sonny knelt on one knee and presented me a small box. When I opened it and saw this beautiful ring, he asked me to marry him. Of course, my answer was yes." Pausing to let her emotions catch up, Tallulah continued. "We held each other for the longest time just watching the sunset, then Sonny picked up a stick and wrote our names in the sand. We walked back to our bungalow down the beach and feasted on ceviche and gallo pinto by candlelight. Afterwards, we were enjoying a cold cerveza when a gentle rain started falling softly on the banana leaves. A chorus of frogs serenaded us as we made passionate love long into the night. We shared a sensory connection that went way beyond any physical pleasure I've ever known. I never knew love could be this wonderful."

"Wow! That's incredible, Tallulah. Costa Rica sounds like a tropical paradise that was the perfect backdrop for saying yes. So, have you two set a date?"

"Not yet, but we're thinking of late spring. Sonny suggested that we get married in the crystal cave. I immediately loved that idea."

"Tallulah, I'm so happy for you two. The cave sounds like an immaculate place for your sacred ceremony."

CHAPTER 38

Love and Forgiveness

Louise was standing on her back porch marveling at the exquisiteness of nature. The cold winter months had finally evolved into a beautiful springtime. Yellow Daffodils, Purple Iris, and fragrant Hyacinths were in bloom, gracing the landscape with their beauty. New sprouts of life were unfurling everywhere—symbolic of new beginnings. Louise opened her book of daily meditations and read the quote for the day.

Great Spirit... To the center of the world you have taken me and showed me the goodness and the beauty and the strangeness of the greening earth...you have shown me and I have seen. Black Elk.

Louise's heart swelled with gratitude.

The renovation of Rolling Waters was near completion. The creamy white of the exterior along with the attractive charcoal color of the trim and shutters made the auspicious red on the front door really stand out. The stained wide-plank flooring on the wrap-around porch added a nice, warm accent.

Louise arranged the rugs and furniture precisely and the art and accessories found their sweet spots. She had chosen an eclectic style with a moderne influence. She was delighted in the contrast of the traditional farm house and the anti-traditional elegance of Art Deco. Rolling Waters turned out better than she could have ever imagined.

Tallulah had painted a beautiful depiction of Rolling Waters and presented it to Hank and Louise as a house-warming present. The farmhouse looked stately, and her brushstrokes created shimmering rays of sunset filtering through the weeping willow. Louise proudly displayed the painting over the fireplace. On the mantel her treasured Roseville vase exhibited an attractive arrangement of Daffodils and Hydrangeas.

On the first of April the final section of the trestle was bolted together and the last spike was driven completing The Shoal Creek Bridge. The bridge was once again open for commerce. As Mr. Wells had promised, the first train was loaded with donations for the coal miners and their families. Charlie was heading up the crew for this historical trip to Thurmond, while Hank and Louise drove their truck. They wanted to make a road trip and take Duchess along. Hank also wanted to stop and visit Nessa and Eileen. Due to his extreme work schedule, he had not been able to talk with his mother in a couple of months. Hank had an uneasy feeling about her.

Their first road trip was fun, but long and tiresome. After traveling many miles, Hank geared down the truck and came to a stop in front of Eileen's house. She rushed outside to greet them both with a big hug. "Hank, I'm really sorry to tell you this, but your mother is gravely ill. The doctor said she has an advanced form of lung cancer. There isn't anything we can do but keep her out of pain." Hank's knees nearly collapsed underneath him, and he grabbed the bed of the truck for support.

"Hank, for Nessa's sake try and pull yourself together. Would you rather see her alone?"

"No. Please, stay with me," Hank answered.

"Darling, look at me. This is going to be hard. Take some deep breaths and try to calm yourself. I'm here for you."

Eileen opened the door, and they followed her inside. Nessa looked very pale. She had lost a lot of weight along with most of her hair. She immediately recognized Hank and held her bony arms up to him. He gingerly embraced her fragile body and said, "Mother! I found Louise and we're back together again. Is there anything we can do?"

Nessa replied in a weakened voice: "A new bahdy perhaps. Hank, I lahve you. I'm 'appy to see dat ye fooehnd Louise." Then she looked at Louise standing in the doorway and motioned for her to come over. She said in her thick Irish accent, "C'mere, me Lassie, 'ow're ye keeping? Me, I'm as seck as a wee 'ahspital. I'm so sahrry fahr bein mean to ya all dahse years. I dahn't know why I acted like dat. Joehst me own insecure self, I guess. Louise, can ye ever fahrgive an ahld dyin wahman?"

Nessa started coughing uncontrollably, and Hank sat on the side of the bed and gently cradled her hacking and rattling body. Louise massaged her hand until she finally settled down.

She offered Nessa a drink of water and said, "Thank you so much, Nessa. I accept your apology. You can leave in peace knowing that Hank and I love each other very much, and we love you, too. Deep down families always love each other—no matter how badly we behave towards one another."

Louise started humming "Take My Hand Precious Lord" in a voice that was very angelic and sweet. Nessa's head was lying on Hank's chest. She smiled at Louise, took one last breath, and then she was gone. Nessa was at peace; love and forgiveness had set her free.

CHAPTER 39

Full Circle

Hank and Louise stood fixated as they stared at the familiar scenery of New River Gorge. They felt like shadow people returning to an old haunt. The meadow, where Louise had picked wildflowers, was the site chosen for the concert. It was a brilliant spring day as the sun beamed brightly from a cloudless sky. Everyone had gathered anticipating the festivities. Charlie was cooking hamburgers on the grill for the crowd. While the young boys were running around playing cowboys and Indians, the girls sat underneath a shade tree playing with their cornhusk dolls.

Hank and Louise made their way to the makeshift stage and were greeted with heartfelt cheers from the crowd. "Thanks, everyone, for coming today. We hope you're having a good time. Over by the big tree, a tent is set up and a volunteer is there to help distribute the clothing, blankets, and numerous other household items. This evening, as we look at your faces, we see old friends and new ones that we haven't met yet. New River Gorge is very nostalgic for Hank and me. We helped season this place with our own blood, sweat, and tears. It will always be a part of who we are. Now, let's cut loose and have some fun."

Louise rosined her bow and started playing "Take It Down From The Mast," an old Irish Civil War song written by James Ryan. The crowd started singing along, and Hank was harmonizing beautifully with his guitar. He took one look at Louise strutting across the stage and felt emotions rise and spill out of him. Michael Coleman's "The Enduring Magic" was the last number of the night.

It had been a perfect day, but the sun was beginning to sink behind the mountains and the air was becoming chilly. Hank spoke in a commanding voice, "Good night, my brothers and sisters. We will never forget you. For those of you who want to continue this party, meet us in the school house. We've brought some mighty fine Tennessee whiskey we'd like to share." Loud cheers erupted from the crowd as Hank and Louise took a bow, then stepped off the stage.

"That was incredible. We did a good thing today," Louise said as they walked away hand in hand.

"Yes, but you should be especially proud. This was your ingenious idea."

"Perhaps, but it would have meant nothing without you. Hank, I know you're concerned about Aunt Eileen. Don't worry, we'll help with the arrangements for your mother. Then we'll talk about her future and what her plans are. Perhaps she might want to come live with us."

"Louise, you have such a good heart, but how is it that you always seem to know what I'm thinking?"

After the fire had burned out and the whiskey was gone, Hank and Louise stayed in one of the miner's cabins similar to their old one. "This is all so surreal. Being here feels like we have come full circle. It makes me so appreciative for the life we now have. Louise, you saved us, and I'll always be grateful to you for getting us out of here."

Louise blew out the kerosene lamp and started massaging Hank's neck and shoulders. She kissed him tenderly and said, "My darling, you've had an emotional couple of days, but tonight I'm going to take you to a place where you will forget about it all."

CHAPTER 40

Walking Through Time

Hank and Louise packed the truck and said their goodbyes. New River Gorge was just a scene in their rearview mirror, but they felt good in knowing that this cold winter everyone would have warm coats and blankets.

They drove back to check on Eileen. A silence and a hauntingly empty feeling greeted them as they entered the house. Hank was still processing the fact that his mother was gone, as well as most all of his family.

"Hank, if there's anything of your mother's that you want, please take it now," Eileen said, breaking the silence.

He looked around the room and said, "I'd like to have this old mirror in the ornate frame. I believe my grandparents brought it over from Ireland. Anything else, please feel free to keep, sell or give away."

"Don't you two worry. I'm gonna be all right. Thanks for your offer of moving to Nashville. I'll let you know what I decide. You kids roll on home safely. Thanks for your love and generosity. I love you two."

The miles clocked on by as the Ford pick-up greedily ate the blacktop. They stopped every couple of hours to stretch, get gas, and change drivers. Duchess had to sniff everything and do her business. They had fallen madly in love with that dog. After the last stop, Hank relinquished control of the wheel and slid down in the seat with his hat over his face. He was too tired to worry about how fast Louise was driving. She loved to drive and eagerly anticipated the next set of Burma Shave signs. The signs were placed far enough apart that passengers had to wait for the next clue. Louise chuckled at the last set. *If you think...she likes...your bristles...walk bare-footed... through some thistles. BURMA SHAVE*

The next morning after breakfast, Louise and Tallulah headed out to *Fanci's Boutique* to pick out a wedding dress. Sadie had changed the name after acquiring the boutique from Carmen.

"Welcome! So, we're looking for a wedding gown? I just received a shipment with an Edward Molyneux gown that is simple yet quite stunning. The gown is made of ivory satin and crepe-de-chine. It's backless and sleeveless and has long sweeping lines. The gown flaunts a beautiful court train that is seeded with pearls." Sadie retrieved the gown and showed it to Tallulah. Louise assisted Tallulah as she tried on the gown. It was exquisite and only needed minor alterations.

"I love this wedding dress. It's plain but sassy. I feel as if it were made just for me," Tallulah said.

"I can't wait 'til Sonny sees you in this gown on your wedding day," Sadie replied.

With all the planning, preparations and excitement, the day of Sonny and Tallulah's wedding arrived. The altar was beautifully decorated with candles, orchids, and palm trees. The dancing flames from the candles illuminated the cave and reflected off the crystal clusters of the natural chandelier. The greenery of the plants was a beautiful and stark contrast to the alien-looking landscape.

The guests were instructed to respect the silence of the cave and not to speak once inside. The only words to be spoken were the exchange of vows. As best man, Charlie stood beside the altar next to Hank and Louise. A Cherokee Medicine Woman was playing a flute as her husband beat hypnotically on a drum. The sound of the flute seemed to spiral through the chambers, and the percussive sound of the drum felt like a pulsing heartbeat of the earth.

It felt as though the moment was somehow preserved and frozen in time. Tallulah entered the chamber and made her way gracefully to the altar—looking incredibly ethereal as if she were walking through time itself. Candlelight reflected and shimmered off her satin gown.

Tallulah approached Sonny and took his hand. He was simply awestruck at her beauty. They smiled and looked into each other's eyes.

Slipping a ring on his finger Tallulah said: "The circle of life shapes us. The circle of light transforms us. This ring represents my never-ending circle of love for you. Sonny, I choose you to be my lover, husband, and friend. Like the circle, stories don't end, they just begin again. This is our story. With an open heart, a soaring spirit, and a sense of absolute gratitude, I take you to be my husband."

Sonny choked up for a moment and fought to regain his composure. He removed the wedding band from his pocket and slipped it on her finger. "The first time I laid eyes on you, my heart whispered, 'She's the one.' My heart was right. From this day forward, I promise to surprise you, amaze you, make you laugh, and love you unconditionally. I give you my hand, my heart, and my word that I will always be a loving and devoted husband. Tallulah, in this sacred place, I take you to be my wife." Sonny kissed her tenderly as salty tears exposed the rawness of their love.

Louise started singing "How Deep Is The Ocean," an Irving Berlin tune. Hank accompanied her on his guitar. The newlyweds silently walked together hand-in-hand out of the cave into the daylight of possibilities.

CHAPTER 41

Sacred Circle of Life

Hank was spinning Louise rather awkwardly across the dance floor of the BirdCage Lounge. The bride and groom had just cut the wedding cake, and the band was playing a lively jazz number. Louise felt a little dizzy from all the champagne she had drunk.

"What's the matter, darling? Are you feeling all right?" Hank asked.

A slow tune ensued, and she laid her head on his shoulder and snuggled closer. "I'm all right. It's getting late. Can we go home?"

The headlights reflected off Rolling Waters as they drove into the driveway. Duchess was barking—excited that her humans were home. Hank opened the door and let her outside. Louise lit a few candles and placed them on the front porch. They sat on the swing, enjoying the night sounds of katydids and crickets as a cool night breeze caressed them. Hoot Owls were serenading the landscape with their mournful calls beneath a waxing moon. Hank put his arm around Louise, and she nestled into him.

"Here's to us and our new home. I really love it here. It's so peaceful in the country," Louise said.

Hank replied tenderly, "My darling, you can't begin to know what a happy man I am right now. Once again, you've done an amazing job decorating our home. You have created magic. Strange, it feels like we've always lived here."

Suspended on creaky chains, they moved slowly back and forth, talking about the wedding and how much life had drastically changed for them since New River Gorge.

Louise leaned into Hank and whispered, "Take me to that place that only you know how to get there."

"I accept that challenge. Come with me." He grabbed an old blanket, and they made their way down to the lake. The moon was reflecting off the water, and the graceful Weeping Willow branches danced seductively in the honeysuckle breeze. Hank sat down on the blanket and removed his clothing. Not waiting for an invitation, Louise slipped out of her dress and seductively straddled Hank. She leaned down and kissed him as he caressed her perfectly formed breasts. He rolled her over and just gazed at her naked beauty reflected in the moonlight. His sensual tongue slowly explored her body as he moved down to her navel. She was moist from sweat and desire, and he was consumed with a fiery passion. The moonlight cast mysterious shadows as they hypnotically rocked until an orgasm washed over them like the waves of an ocean.

Hank and Louise were enjoying breakfast on the back porch the next morning while discussing their upcoming schedules. Due to Hank's exemplary work on the bridge project, Mr. Johnson reassigned him as conductor on the Nashville to Chicago passenger train. His schedule was four days on and three off. Hank was appreciative of the promotion and raise, but he missed the thrust of power from engaging the locomotive's throttle.

As Louise was clearing the table, they heard the unmistakable sound of Sonny's Harley thundering up the driveway. Duchess started barking and ran to greet him. Sonny killed the rumbling engine and placed the kickstand down as Louise walked down the steps. "Good morning, newlywed. What brings you out to the country this morning?"

Sonny walked up on the porch and shook Hank's hand. Directing his next comment to Louise, he said, "I can't stay long, because Tallulah is home packing for our honeymoon to Niagara Falls. Louise, I had to personally come and tell you the good news. A rep from the Grand Ole Opry contacted me, and they would like for you to perform on October 24. What do you think about that? It seems, my lady, that you have become quite popular."

Louise leaned against Hank thinking she might faint at the good news. "Oh! Sonny, I just can't believe it. Dreams really do come true." She looked up at Hank and said, "Who would have ever thought when we were listening to The Grand Ole Opry in New River Gorge that I would be singing there one day?"

Hank just smiled and said, "For one—me. I've always believed you were good enough to be on that stage."

Sonny continued, "Also, I want to see if May 13 would be a good date to reschedule your makeup concert in Chicago. I think this would be an ideal place to launch your new album—*Wings Of Destiny.*"

Louise replied, "Yes. Those dates work fine." She addressed Hank, "Looks like I'll be riding the rails with you to Chicago."

Sonny said goodbye and roared down the long drive, kicking up dust, as Duchess happily escorted him to the gate.

On Thursday afternoon, Louise was at the depot waiting for Hank. She loved the sight of her man rolling into the station waving like a schoolboy. Hank jumped down from the train, then picked Louise up and swung her around. He put his arm around her as they walked to the truck. "Hey! Woman! Do you think that perhaps I might be able to drive the truck home?" She just laughed and pitched him the keys.

The Chicago concert was explosive. With Hank by her side, Louise's experience with the Windy City was much more enjoyable. *Wings Of Destiny* received rave reviews. Requests for bookings came pouring in.

As the summer months rolled by, Hank and Louise settled into a comfortable routine at Rolling Waters. Louise loved to dig in the dirt and had become rather proficient with gardening. One of her passions was growing herbs. She loved picking fresh herbs from the garden for cooking and inviting friends over for supper.

One morning in late September, Louise took Hank to the station for a Chicago run. She had not been feeling well, but chose not to mention anything to him just yet. Louise had a meeting with the manager of the Grand Ole Opry and decided that perhaps she would go visit the doctor afterwards for a check-up. She thought, *Something is just not quite right.*

Louise was standing on the platform waiting for Hank to come home from a Chicago run. He arrived a little late, but as usual he lifted Louise and swung her around. She felt dizzy and grabbed for some real estate to stop the spin.

"Are you all right, Louise?"

She just smiled and handed him the keys. When they arrived home, Louise suggested to Hank that he bathe and change clothes. While he was doing so, she finished the final preparations for supper. The table on the back porch was beautifully set. Candles flamed beside her Roseville vase filled with exotic passion flowers—Tennessee's official state wildflower.

Hank walked out, looking refreshed and sexy in a pair of blue jeans and a white linen shirt. Louise could not resist the sight of him. She walked over and gave him a kiss, and then escorted him to the table.

They sat down to eat, and Hank remarked, "Hey! Why am I the only one with a drink?"

Louise stared intently towards the tranquil lake, taking her time in answering. As she was enjoying the beauty of the sunset, a loud trumpeting sound resonated across the land. A flock of Sandhill Cranes landed at the lake on their annual migration from Alaska. Duchess wanted to go after them, but Hank held her back. Silently, they marveled at the behavior of the long-legged birds that proudly displayed a six-foot wing span. The brilliant red on their heads accented the black, white and greyish plumage. Come dawn, the flock will leave their overnight roost, once again, filling the sky with their spectacular elegance.

Finally, Louise took Hank's hand and looked sadly into his blue eyes. "Hank, I have something to tell you. I haven't been feeling well, so while you were gone I went to the doctor and had a checkup."

Alarm registered on Hank's face. He asked with great concern, "Darling, what's wrong?"

She paused for a moment with her head hanging low. Louise looked at him with misty eyes. "Hank O'Neill, I'm not having a drink, because I'm having our baby instead."

Hank jumped up in disbelief and embraced her. "Louise! Louise! What exciting news! I'm so happy, darling. We're gonna have a baby! And if you can't drink, I promise, neither will I. Woman, you're so bad. You really scared the hell out of me there for a second."

Louise flashed Hank a mischievous grin, "Sorry, I couldn't resist messing with ya. Hank, I have found my home with you. You make me laugh, and you allow me to cry. You complete me. I'm so happy! We're gonna be a family."

Hank placed a hand gently on her belly. "My home is wherever you are, my darling. I can't wait to welcome our little one into this world. "

They kissed passionately temporarily lost in the magic of the moment. Orange, red and indigo clouds reflected the sun's light and drifted lazily across the majestic sky. At last, the grandeur of the sunset faded into twilight—that enchanted time between dark and light where anything is possible. A shooting star flamed across the sky as it streaked through the earth's atmosphere. With a vast sense of wonder, Louise held Hank's hand and thought, *It's nature's design to take and give back life. The unknown unfurls as we journey around the sacred circle of life. Each breath is a gift, and my heart is filled with gratitude for this moment and the mysterious future yet to come.*

THE END ... THE BEGINNING ...

ACKNOWLEDGEMENTS

It is with much appreciation that I offer my heartfelt thanks to Rose Phillips for her editing and mentoring skills. Rose's continued encouragement gave me confidence to think outside the box, do the hard work, and go deeper.

A special thanks to Kathy McClelland for her editorial expertise and encouragement.

Thanks to Marianne Terry for your humor and optimism. The wolf is dead because of you

I am grateful to Crescent River Port Pilot, Abel Strickland, for sharing knowledge of the Mississippi River in New Orleans.

Thank you, Bill Welder, for creating the fabulous art chosen for the cover of this book. Your art is inspirational. Keep your creativity going and inspire others.

My most intimate gratitude goes to Tim, my handsome husband, for challenging me to write this book. Bill Welder's Tracks to Nowhere spurred many conservations on hot August nights while enjoying mango margaritas. Hank and Louise were born from those hot nights, as an idea that manifested. Tim, my love, thanks for your passion and unwavering belief in me, even when, at times, I only had doubts.

Finally, if this book has found its way into your hands, then dear reader, I thank you.

Sharon Vogt

AUTHOR'S NOTES

Tracks from Nowhere is my debut novel at the age of sixty-nine years young, proving the old adage "You are never too old to set another goal or to dream a new dream." The idea for this book began when I first saw Bill Welder's *Tracks to Nowhere* in a gallery in Asheville, North Carolina. My imagination inspired me to ask the questions, "Where is he headed? What is his story?"

Nonchalantly, my husband Tim simply replied, "Well then, why don't write it." After much time and dedication, I am pleased to offer my story graced with Bill's art on the cover.

"Bring Back the Sunshine and Roses" was written by my mother, Louise Lancaster, to my father, Albert Sprouse, in November of 1933 shortly before their marriage. He was serving in the Civilian Conservation Corps, which was founded by President Roosevelt to combat high unemployment during the Great Depression.

Liquor-by-the-drink was not available in Nashville, Tennessee until 1967. In order to make a more interesting scenario, I took the liberty of creating a whiskey, neon Nashville reminiscent of today's vibrant downtown.

Having grown up in Littleton, Alabama, beside a railroad track, trains have always fascinated me and have been an intrinsic part of my life. In fact, I wrote a majority of this book while traveling on trains from San Francisco to Denver and Birmingham to New York. If you love trains too, then I sincerely hope that you enjoy this journey on the *Tracks from Nowhere*.